Some people were gluttons for punishment. Stupid people. Sure enough, they fit the category. The man sprinted toward Gaia, fists swinging.

It was pitiful. Gaia almost felt like laughing. But she was too pissed off. The stupid ones were always the worst fighters. Gaia stepped sideways. There was no reason to engage him. As she dodged the guy's fists, the force of his own weight made him stumble. He fell toward the ground, and Gaia heard a popping sound in his wrist as he tried to catch himself with his left hand.

Logically, Gaia knew that she should probably feel *some* semblance of fear right now. Sure, she was winning the battle. Even so, deserted park plus attacking mugger equals fear.

But all she felt was another surge of adrenaline.

For orders other than by individual consumers, Pocket Books grants a discount on the purchase of 10 or more copies of single titles for special markets or premiums, etc. For further details, please write to the Vice-President of Special Markets, Pocket Books, 1230 Avenue of the Americas, New York, NY 10020-1586, 8th Floor.

For information on how individual consumers can place orders, please write to Mail Order Department, Simon & Schuster Inc., 100 Front Street, Riverside, NJ 08075.

Don't miss any books in this thrilling series:

FEARLESS™

Available from POCKET PULSE

FEARLESS™

BAD

FRANCINE PASCAL

POCKET PULSE

New York London Toronto Sydney Singapore

To William Rubin

An *Original* Publication of POCKET BOOKS

POCKET PULSE, published by
Pocket Books, a division of Simon & Schuster, Inc.
1230 Avenue of the Americas, New York, NY 10020

Produced by 17th Street Productions,
an Alloy Online, Inc. company
33 West 17th Street
New York, NY 10011

Copyright © 2001 by Francine Pascal

Cover art copyright © 2001 by 17th Street Productions,
an Alloy Online, Inc. company.
Cover photography by St. Denis. Cover design by Mike Rivilis.

ISBN: 0-7434-1247-8

First Pocket Pulse Paperback printing January 2001

10 9 8 7 6 5 4 3 2 1

Fearless™ is a trademark of Francine Pascal.
POCKET PULSE and colophon are
trademarks of Simon & Schuster, Inc.

Printed in the U.S.A.

BAD

Gaia and Sam. Sam and Gaia.

I never thought I'd see those two names together.

Sam and *me*. Yes, me. Gaia Moore. A poorly dressed Xena, Warrior Princess, minus the sex appeal and cult following. It's impossible to believe. After everything that happened—after all the lies and betrayal and death and just plain old bull- shit—it's beyond miraculous. It's out there in biblical, apocalyp- tic, here-comes-the-rapture ter- ritory.

People always talk about kismet. You know, the idea that two people are destined to be together—and they'll eventually find each other, no matter what bizarre, horrendous paths they may take. And I've always put kismet right up there with UFOs and the tooth fairy on the believability scale.

But now . . . I don't know.

When Sam found me in the park, I honestly felt like I was being

visited by some kind of appari-
tion. A phantom, conjured out of
my subconscious. He was literally
the last person I expected to
see. For once I hadn't even been
thinking about him. No, my mind
was definitely somewhere else.
There's nothing like nearly getting killed and then seeing your
foster mother murdered to dis-
tract you from your obsession.

Then, when Sam started to
apologize for everything that had
happened between us—for Ella, for
the misunderstandings, for how
he'd failed—I wondered if the
bullet hadn't missed me after
all. For a split second I honestly thought I had died. And
that's a pretty big deal because
I don't believe in the afterlife.
(I don't believe in much at all,
actually, but that's another
story.) But I especially don't
believe in some great spirit
world, some ethereal plane beyond
our reach.

Still, at that moment, I have

to admit, I had my doubts. After all, I was experiencing my version of heaven. There was Sam Moon, standing before me at the Pearly Gates (okay, at the miniature Arc de Triomphe in Washington Square Park, but close enough), telling me everything I'd always dreamed of him saying.

And it was all real. When he put his arms around me, I knew I wasn't hallucinating. For one thing, he accidentally stepped on my toe—hard. It was like pinching yourself on the arm to make sure you're awake. Plus I never cry in my dreams. And we cried that night. About a lot of things. About Ella, whom neither of us ever even really knew . . . the Ella who ended up finding her true self in the last moments of her life because she realized she had been used—used by a monster far more sick than I had ever imagined *her* being.

But I don't want to think about that. I don't want to think

about all the people I've lost,
like my mother, or Ella, or my
best friend, Mary. There's no
point in dwelling on the nega-
tive. Not anymore. Because mostly
Sam and I talked about the time
we missed out on being together
because we can both be complete
assholes.

Then we kissed.

To be honest, I can't remember
much else.

They say that there are only two things a person can ever be sure of: death and taxes. Having never paid taxes myself, I'm not even sure of that one. But I'm sure of one thing: Gaia Moore.

It's funny. Not "ha-ha" funny, either. More like the kind of funny that makes your insides twist into a horrible, sickening knot—because since the moment I saw her, my life has been a Tilt-A-Whirl. For example: My grades dropped, I was kidnapped, I broke up with my perfect, desirable, beautiful girlfriend, and I have reason to believe that I've developed an ulcer. And that's just for starters.

But it's all been worth it. Describing my feelings has never been my strong point, but I have to say, when I'm in a four-mile radius of Gaia, nothing else exists. Nothing. Yes, that's a terrible, simpleminded cliché, but it's actually true. Nuclear war? Who cares? The bubonic plague is headed for New York? So what? I'll stay inside. I felt that way the very first time it happened—even before I knew her, and I can't explain why.

I've spent countless hours thinking about Gaia, trying to figure out what it is about her that makes me risk life and limb to be close to her for even a minute. I've come to the conclusion that she isn't human. I don't know if she's an angel, an alien, a sprite, or an oversize leprechaun. But she's definitely not of this earth.

I knew it for sure when I actually had Gaia in my arms. If I could just hold her on a steady basis for about a week, I would die a happy man. But maybe I won't have to die to get my wish. Maybe, just maybe, Gaia and I actually have a shot at being together.

If it works out—even for a week or less—then everything bad that's happened will be null and void in my mind. Life will be perfect. . . .

Except for one thing.

My friend Mike Suarez is in the hospital, and he might die.

But that can't happen. No. Not when my life has the potential to be so good. Please, God, don't let that happen.

She could feel the exhaustion creeping over her, smothering her like one of those lead **cold** blankets **and** people have to **lifeless** wear in an X-ray room. Her knees buckled. Her eyesight dimmed.

THE MAN AT THE MORGUE WAS

Overly Made-up Nympho

straight out of central casting. Pale, bloated face, long, skinny fingers, creepy black eyes. He actually *grinned* at Gaia as he pulled Ella's body out of the morgue's special refrigeration system. Gaia wasn't afraid of the guy—she was never afraid—but it didn't take too much imagination to picture the kind of things he might do after hours to the corpses in his care.

"Can you identify this woman, Ms. Moore?" the man asked, flicking his gaze over Gaia's body before raising his eyebrows at her.

"Her name is Ella. I mean . . . it *was* Ella. Ella Niven."

It sounded to Gaia as if her voice were coming from a speaker in some other room: fake, distant. *Everything* about the moment seemed fake—the harsh, fluorescent lights, the antiseptic stink of chemicals, the cold metal surfaces—everything, in fact, except the film of sweat forming over the pathologist's upper lip. *Ella* certainly didn't look real. Her skin was a sort of light blue-gray color, and her lips were completely white because of all the blood she had lost. Her dyed red hair had been pushed away from her face, and it resembled the kind of cheap clown wigs they sold on Bleecker Street.

Gaia thought Ella would at least appear as if she were finally at peace. People always said that about the dead. But Ella just looked . . . lifeless. Cold and lifeless.

Creepy Guy smiled again, holding out a form for Gaia to sign.

And then it was over.

The next thing Gaia knew, she was running down Seventh Avenue, determined to put as much space as she could between herself and the basement of St. Vincent's Hospital. Sometimes New York City just wasn't big enough. Her thoughts swirled like dead leaves breaking into fragments in an autumn wind. One more person was out of her life. Like her mother. Like Mary. Ella Niven was officially no more. Gaia was minus one foster mother.

A month ago, even a week ago, Gaia would have been happy to see Ella buried six feet under. The woman had done everything possible to make Gaia's life a living hell. Including sleeping with Sam Moon. But then—

Gaia took a right onto Christopher Street, skidding for a moment on the cold pavement. She dashed across the street, barely registering a splash into one of those slush puddles that guaranteed wet socks and frozen toes. At least it was a little warmer than it had been. It was already almost February, after all. Spring would be here soon. Gaia couldn't wait for the spring. . . .

Maybe she should just stop thinking about Ella. Right. The coming spring meant making a fresh start. She should stop thinking about the past—and in particular, about what she'd learned of Ella in the past few days. Her stepmother hadn't been a plastic, overly made-up nymphomaniac with an IQ of twenty. No. The *real* Ella had been a master of the martial arts, intelligent, and incredibly complicated.

Just like me. Well, maybe except for the intelligent part. But otherwise . . .

After another skidding turn, the Nivens' Perry Street brownstone swam out of the wintry darkness, like it had so many times in the past. The windows were dark. Lifeless. The place was deserted, a tomb. Gaia swallowed as she bounded up the steps, her wet sneakers slapping on the smooth stone. If she'd never thought of this place as home before, she didn't know *what* to think of it now.

She slid her key into the dead-bolt lock and opened the door. The house was cold; not that this was any big surprise. Gaia felt as if she hadn't been here in a year. It was strange; she had been here twice today already—once to receive the call from the man at the morgue. The house had been cold then, too.

Even a week ago she would have been thrilled to

11

come into the brownstone and discover that she had the place to herself. But now as she stood in the narrow hallway by the ticking grandfather clock, she realized that it felt less like a tomb and more like a movie set. In a way it *was* a set, a stage. A fake family had lived here, leading fake lives.

She started up the creaky staircase, averting her gaze from the cheesy photos that Ella had taken to enhance her image as a dumb bimbo. It was harder than ever to believe that Ella's husband, George—ironically, an old CIA buddy of her dad's—had insisted that this would be a *real* home. A place for Gaia to finally grow some roots after all those years of bouncing from one foster home to another . . . after her mom's death and her dad's disappearance.

A bitter bile rose in her throat. Gaia wouldn't think of her dad. Never again. *He* had engineered the destruction that had nearly consumed her.

Mary Moss would have found something funny about this situation, Gaia thought as her footsteps pounded up the stairs. *She would have provided some old-fashioned gallows humor to make me laugh. . . .*

But Mary had met the same fate as Ella. She had been assassinated. Every time Gaia thought of the sleazy drug dealer's henchman who had taken Mary's life, she felt like punching her fist through a wall—or better yet, through an assassin's face. She shook her head as she reached the fourth-floor landing. She still wasn't sure *why* Ella had sacrificed herself to the assassin's bullet, why Ella had claimed that *she* was Gaia. Or maybe she just didn't want to dwell on it. The tears that Gaia had shed when she saw Ella's dead body had been real. She'd hated her foster mother for so long—and in the end, she'd seen the truth. They were kindred spirits. They were both utterly lost. . . .

So maybe there was some humor in the situation. After all, when Gaia had first moved in, George had hoped that Ella would be a surrogate mother to her. Ha! It really would have been funny if it wasn't so pitiful and sad. For all she knew, George *still* believed that Ella had married him for love, that she'd had no hidden agenda, that she hadn't been mixed up with something twisted and evil and cruel. It was amazing, actually. How could somebody be so blind? Ella had done everything from "forget" to give Gaia phone messages, to sleep with Sam, to order a hit on Gaia's life.

On the other hand, Gaia knew all about willful blindness. She'd been wearing shades three feet thick for the first twelve years of her life. She hadn't caught a glimpse of her own father's true nature—

You're not going to think about him.

No. She had a new family now. She had Sam. She had her uncle. Oliver. Well, maybe she had Oliver. He'd promised to take her away—then vanished as abruptly as he'd appeared. But she was certain he would contact her again. He *had* to. There was just no predicting when or how. Not with him.

And there was one more family member, too— one more member of the odd and disparate little unit of people Gaia had allowed herself to become close with. There was Ed Fargo. But then, Ed might be another "maybe" as well. He'd been there from the very start, wheeling around the back-ground of her life when she didn't know a soul aside from the freakish chess players in the park . . . but now he was spending *way* too much time with Heather Gannis. In fact, now that Gaia really thought about it, Ed had become the first male FOH. The first Friend of Heather's who didn't wear lipstick. (Although who knew what Heather made him do when they were alone together?)

A smirk curled on Gaia's lips. What Ed needed was a good dose of reality. Some wheelchair jokes and Krispy Kreme doughnuts. The kind of thing Heather would never provide.

Gaia sighed, reaching the fourth-floor landing. The door of her room groaned as she pushed it open. In the shadows the bedroom looked the same as it had the last time she'd been in it. It felt the same, too. Like a hotel room. Like a place to crash, but not a place where she belonged. It was temporary. It always had been. Gaia flicked on the light and began to throw items of clothing onto her bed.

Somewhere between the front door and the door of her bedroom, she had made a decision. She wouldn't stay in this house another day. Not another *second*. There was no reason. Even if her uncle Oliver didn't take her away, as he'd promised . . . well, she could always stay with Sam. Of course she could. She had to tell him about Oliver, anyway, about the possibility that she might be leaving New York for a while. Item by item the sum total of her possessions—her *life*—went into her ratty duffel bag: her cargo pants, her T-shirts and sweatshirts, the clothes that hung off her frame like potato sacks but still somehow couldn't conceal the muscles. . . .

But who cared about her bulging biceps and thunder thighs? Sam liked the way she looked. That was all that mattered.

It took Gaia all of seven minutes to gather everything. She left the pair of Gap capri pants she had bought during a moment of temporary insanity hanging in the closet. Then she swung her duffel bag over her shoulder and opened the bedroom window. She wanted to leave this house the way she had most often when Ella was alive. She would climb out of the window. She would escape.

A final tribute to Ella, she thought, throwing her leg over the sill. *A very fitting tribute.*

15

WAS THERE SOME CITY ORDINANCE

stating that all SoHo boutiques had to be smaller than a hundred square feet?

Ed Fargo drummed his fingers restlessly on his baggy jeans. This was the third place he and Heather had hit this

A Little PG-13 Fun

afternoon, and he was starting to feel extremely claustrophobic—especially since his wheelchair seemed to fill up half the room. Maybe that was why every woman who worked in these stores maintained the weight of a life-size cardboard cutout. If they were actually three-dimensional, they wouldn't be able to fit.

"How are we doing in there?" the saleswoman called, rapping on the dressing-room door. Her name was Simone. It figured. She pronounced it "see-moooane." And there was another thing all SoHo saleswomen had in common: They favored the royal "we." Probably so they could convince customers that "we" needed to spend three hundred and fifty dollars on a tank top.

"I'll be out in a minute," came Heather's muffled reply.

Ed ran his hand through his scruffy brown hair and glanced around the shop, frowning. Another minute and he might go crazy and start trashing the place. But he had woken up this morning with a mission. He was going to buy Heather Gannis an incredibly sexy, absurdly expensive new dress. No matter what the cost.

Yeah, the mission was sort of cheesy. Yeah, it was the kind of thing that only happened in those lame teen movies that seemed to come out every single week, the ones with titles like, *You Go, Girl!* or, *That's So Five Minutes Ago!* But under the circumstances, a little PG-13 teen fun was just fine. Heather needed a pick-me-up in the same way Ed needed . . . well, best not to go there.

Her sister, Phoebe, was barely clinging to life after a bout with anorexia. Heather had just broken up with her old boyfriend, Sam Moon (not that Ed was particularly upset about *that*, of course), and on a more practical level, Ed was one of the few people outside of her immediate family who knew that the Gannis family was currently broke. Heather's life was shit. No doubt about it.

"One more second," Heather called.

"Okay." Simone glanced nervously in Ed's direction. "Would you and your, uh, friend like something to drink?" she asked the closed door. "Perrier? Evian?"

"Nothing for me, thanks," Heather answered.

Ed resisted the urge to snort. Naturally, the

saleswoman assumed that Heather was just a "friend." She couldn't conceive that a girl who looked like Heather could possibly want to go out with a guy in a wheelchair. Then again, sometimes it was hard for Ed to believe that, too. Two months ago he would have said that he and Heather had as much of a chance of getting back together as Tommy Lee and Pamela Anderson.

"You know, she's my sister, actually," he announced to Simone. "We were twins joined at birth. After the operation, she ended up with the spinal cord."

The woman's eyes narrowed, but she smiled politely. And he had to hand it to her; that was a better reaction than most people could muster. Definitely. Most people either looked sick or simply ran off. Oh, yes. He knew all about people running off. Like Heather herself. She had done just that two years ago—right after the accident. And the fact that she had been completely in love with him *before* the accident didn't matter. Nope. As soon as Heather saw Ed in the wheelchair, she'd disappeared. Not literally, of course. She'd been right there, in his face, every single day at school, but Ed simply had to watch her from the sidelines.

But that was the past. He wouldn't allow himself to get bitter over it. Because one day a few weeks ago Ed had glimpsed the *old* Heather. It was literally as if she'd stepped out of a fog. Gone were all the hang-ups and hangers-on, those "FOHs," as Gaia Moore liked to call them. And then, after a few very bizarre and clumsy encounters—particularly one involving a strange and impulsive make-out session in a storage room at the Plaza Hotel—they suddenly found themselves falling back into their old relationship. And not a moment too soon. Because before that, Ed had been driving himself crazy with daily fantasies starring . . . well, none other than the FOH hater herself: Gaia Moore.

But there was no point in thinking about *her*. Especially not now.

Luckily, the dressing-room door happened to burst open at that second.

"Ta-da!" Heather exclaimed, strolling out into the shop.

Ed blinked. "Uh . . . wow," he mumbled. *Brilliant compliment there, Fargo.* But it was by far the best he could manage, seeing as he was about to start drooling at any second. Heather's shiny dark hair tumbled over the straps of the red dress, and the neckline plunged low, revealing a hint of cleavage. The bottom barely cleared her knees. Ed's eyes roved up and down her body, eventually settling on her hips. The red fabric clung to them quite nicely.

Heather smiled, pivoting in front of a mirror. "I

take it that means you like it," she stated wryly. Her amber-streaked eyes shone as she checked herself out.

Suddenly Ed found himself reaching for her hand. "Kiss me," he whispered.

She glanced down at him, her brow furrowing. "What? Here?"

"Yeah," he said, affecting a macho slouch. "And make it good."

For a second she stared at him. Her eyes darted to Simone. Then she started laughing. "You're weird, Fargo."

He shrugged. "I'm waiting."

Heather's smile widened. Ed's heart picked up a beat. He was joking, sure. But it was strange; this was the very first time he actually felt in *charge*, in *control* with her—the way he had when he'd been able to use his legs and jump and skate and dance. He wasn't even conscious of the chair. At least, not until she leaned forward and put her arms around his neck, sliding her fingers—

Simone cleared her throat.

Heather pulled away, grinning wryly.

So much for the moment. Then again, this wasn't exactly a darkened storage room at the Plaza Hotel. Ed sighed and turned to the saleswoman.

"We'll take the dress," he said.

Heather's jaw dropped. She started shaking her

head. "No way. I was just trying it on. Ed, this dress costs, like, four hundred bucks—"

"I told you I was going to buy you a dress today," he interrupted. "So let me get this for you."

"But I . . ." Heather bit her lip.

Poor Heather, he thought. With him, at least, she never tried to hide her feelings. Ed could practically see the thoughts racing through her brain, as if they were posted on some kind of electronic billboard. (*a*) She didn't want to take advantage of him. (*b*) She really wanted something new. (*c*) She hadn't actually *bought* a new item of clothing in several months. For Heather, that was like going without oxygen.

"Heather, come on," he prodded. "I insist. It's no big deal."

And it wasn't. No, sir. Not that Heather had any real idea of Ed's financial status. But he had twenty-six million bucks coming his way. The accident might have robbed him of his legs—but he'd be able to buy as many dresses in as many boutiques as Heather wanted. And that counted for something. Didn't it?

"Okay," she said finally. She winked. "But I want to figure out a way to pay you back." She paused dramatically. "An *imaginative* way."

"Uh . . . s-sounds good," he stammered. He could feel blood rushing to his face as he rolled to the cash register. Maybe he wasn't as in control with her as he would have liked to believe. But it was always nice to pretend.

THE STUFFED DUFFEL BAG KNOCKED

against Gaia's hip as she headed toward Washington Square Park. The strap dug into her shoulder. But the pain didn't bother her.

The Drill

She was on her way to Sam's dorm room. *Nothing* could bother her.

It was closing in on five o'clock, and the sun was long hidden behind the apartment buildings on the West Side. A chilly wind swept through the leafless trees. Gaia picked up her pace. Aside from a few joggers and NYU students, the park was nearly empty. Surprisingly, even the chess tables were deserted. But that was fine with her. Fewer people around meant fewer slow-moving bodies to dodge on her way to meet Sam.

In ten minutes Sam would get out of his last class of the day, and Gaia would meet him in front of his dorm. They would go up to his room. They would be *together*. Again, for the hundredth time that day, she felt like this was happening to someone else, that this couldn't be part of *her* life . . . a life pretty much defined by misery, with an occasional ass kicking thrown in—doled out by Gaia to various sick and depraved individuals.

Gaia felt a strange stirring deep inside her gut. It wasn't nervousness, exactly. And it sure as hell wasn't fear. But what was it? Her imagination swirled with images of Sam. A smile crept over her lips. And then she knew: It was the feeling a girl got when she was about to go meet her boyfriend, when she didn't know what was going to happen. When the possibilities were literally limitless, when she felt a tingling in certain parts of her body . . .

Her eyes fell on the stone chess tables as she cruised past them. *That's where I met him,* she thought. He'd sat down—right there, right at this very spot—to play a game of pickup chess. It had been one of those defining moments that change everything. She'd hated him from afar, but only because he was so gorgeous. And then she'd discovered he was an amazing chess player. Brilliant. But they had never finished the game. Rain started to pour from the sky, and Sam had disappeared—

A faint scrap of conversation tore into her thoughts.

Her head jerked up. *Russian.*

Standing by the miniature Arc de Triomphe on the north side of the park was a young couple huddled together, studying an unwieldy map. For a brief moment Gaia's heart squeezed. Every time she heard the language, she pictured her mother's face. Her mother had taught Gaia her native tongue from the time she was a baby. And Gaia had clung to it, treasuring it as the only real link between her and the woman who had brought her into this world.

The couple glanced up at Gaia as she approached and offered a tentative smile.

Oh, brother. Gaia sighed, thrusting the thoughts of her mother from her mind. She knew the type: young travelers from abroad, determined to see each and every New York City landmark no matter how low the temperature dropped. The drill was always the same, too. They would probably ask her how to get to ten different places, then start off in the exact opposite direction of where Gaia had suggested.

"Hello?" the woman called out, waving.

Now that Gaia was close, she could see that the couple probably wasn't much older than twenty-two. They were scruffy, alternative types, the kind of kids who knew nothing of the States but probably loved watching American MTV.

"Please—you help us, tell us where we go?" the man asked Gaia, gesturing toward the map.

Gaia nodded. *"Zdrastvooytye,"* she said: Russian for "hello."

The couple's jaws dropped. They exchanged a shocked glance.

Gaia smiled. *Bet you didn't think I could do that, huh?* "Where do you want to go?" she asked, continuing in Russian. It was nice to know her accent was still flawless.

"The Empire State Building," the woman answered.

"It's easy," Gaia stated. "Go east to Christopher Street. Take the number-one train to Thirty-fourth Street. . . ." Her voice trailed off as she noticed that both of their expressions were still totally baffled. Obviously they had no idea what she was talking about. She might as well have still been speaking in English.

"See where I'm pointing?" Gaia asked, turning toward Fourth Street.

The woman hovered at Gaia's side, craning her neck to look down the street. *How has this couple managed to get along without running into someone who happens to speak Russian?* Gaia wondered impatiently. Talk about clueless. At this rate she would be late to meet Sam. "Walk toward those benches—"

There was a tugging at her arm. It was hard. Aggressive.

What the hell?

An alarm went off in Gaia's brain. She turned quickly. The Russian guy's hand was gripping the strap of Gaia's messenger bag, and his feet were poised to run. Unbelievable! So the helpless tourist couple apparently weren't quite so helpless. Assholes. Anger

25

surged through her veins, along with the electric fizzle she always felt before combat. Her hand instantly clamped down on the guy's forearm.

"Big mistake, jerk," Gaia muttered in Russian.

She took a step back with her right foot, then spun to her left with a quick kung fu move that wrenched the guy's arm—painfully.

"*Aiee!*" he cried.

His fingers slipped from the strap of the bag. He staggered backward.

Gaia's eyes flashed to the woman. *Damn it.* She wasn't in the mood for a fight. Not now. She had to meet Sam. She couldn't afford to keel over with exhaustion and wind up face first on the pavement, either. Fearlessness came with a price: She was always sapped of strength after kicking someone's ass. Hopefully, though, this would be the end of this pathetic attempted mugging.

But it appeared that the couple was a tag team. As soon as the mister was out of range, the missus lunged forward and scratched at Gaia's face.

Instinctively Gaia pivoted and knocked the woman's hand away from her face. Then in one swift motion she kicked the woman in the stomach, sending her toppling to the ground.

Don't complain, Gaia thought as the woman moaned. *That could have hurt a lot worse.* She fell into a traditional karate stance, looking from the man to the woman, wondering if they were going to be stupid enough to take one more grab at her bag. Some people were gluttons for punishment. Stupid people. Sure enough, they fit the category. The man sprinted toward Gaia, fists swinging.

It was pitiful. Gaia almost felt like laughing. But she was too pissed off. The stupid ones were always the worst fighters. Gaia stepped sideways. There was no reason to engage him. As she dodged the guy's fists, the force of his own weight made him stumble. He fell toward the ground, and Gaia heard a popping sound in his wrist as he tried to catch himself with his left hand.

Logically, Gaia knew that she should probably feel *some* semblance of fear right now. Sure, she was winning the battle. Even so, deserted park plus attacking mugger equals fear. But all she felt was another surge of adrenaline.

"Bitch!" the guy yelled in English, staggering to his feet.

Gaia frowned. There was barely a trace of an accent. Who *were* these people? Did they pretend to be foreigners to get their victims to let their guards down . . . so they could pick on easy prey? Her jaw tightened. Now she was *more* than pissed. She glanced toward the woman, who was backing away, obviously slightly smarter than her counterpart. But

27

the guy was still stumbling toward her. Gaia took aim, then punched the man once in the abdomen. She could hear the breath whooshing out of his lungs. He slumped to the ground, clutching his stomach.

"Let's go!" the woman shrieked.

With a last angry glance the man turned and stumbled toward the east exit of the park. The woman hobbled after him.

Gaia shook her head, scowling. She could feel the exhaustion creeping over her, smothering her like one of those lead blankets people have to wear in an X-ray room. Her knees buckled. Her eyesight dimmed. *Shit!* she thought furiously. Why hadn't the cops been anywhere in sight? The New York City police department really needed to do something to make this park a safer place. Gaia seemed to be the only one ready, willing, and able to deal with scumbags. And it was getting a little more than tiresome. Especially now that she had better things to do. Like getting into bed with Sam Moon.

Unfortunately, that would have to wait. Because at that moment Gaia found herself plopping down on her butt. She stared vacantly into space, feeling very much like somebody had just removed her internal batteries.

Soon I'll be out of here, she thought bitterly. *Soon Oliver will give me a break from all this crap.*

HE WAS FOND OF THIS NEW PLACE.

The Same DNA

The Upper West Side two bedroom was more modest than the apartments he'd previously used as home base. But he was pleased that there were two Columbia professors living on his floor. Despite his unusual lifestyle, Loki thought of himself as something of an academic. Maybe he would accept the political science professor's invitation to come over for coffee one afternoon. The man would undoubtedly be impressed with Loki's vast knowledge of world affairs.

Loki smiled. Of course he wouldn't accept the invitation. He couldn't afford to interact with outsiders. Loneliness often gave rise to foolish thoughts. But that was all they were: thoughts. He was far too experienced to let them interfere with his job. He knew far too well that every single person was a potential enemy—even a man in a tweed jacket and a shabby green turtleneck.

I won't be lonely for much longer, though, Loki thought.

No. He picked up one of the many untraceable cell phones he kept in his possession and walked to the large picture window on the west side of his living room. His gaze swept out over the Hudson River—across Riverside

Park to the glittering lights of New Jersey. So may people crammed into such a small space. Were any of them as lonely as he was?

Loki punched one of the speed dial buttons.

Before the first ring had finished, a German voice answered. "Hello?"

"She's passed her final test," Loki stated in German. "We are ready to proceed with the plan."

"Yes, sir. I understand."

"I want everything in place. I want the facility secured. This is *imperative*. We'll be leaving the country within the week."

"Yes, sir," the voice on the other end answered again. He sounded bored. "I understand."

"If anything goes wrong, I will cut you open and make you eat your own intestines before you die," Loki stated simply.

There was no response.

"Do you understand *that?*" Loki demanded.

"Yes, sir. I—"

Loki hung up the phone. These young operatives disgusted him. Either they didn't give him the proper respect, or they were completely submissive. Some would shoot themselves in the head if Loki ordered them to do so. Others, like the fool with whom he'd just spoken, resented him.

But they all feared him. Fear kept them in line.

Soon it will be just the two of us, though.

Yes. Just him and her. Loki and Gaia. No more servants or subordinates. Gaia Moore was the one woman on earth who had the potential to be his equal. She was the daughter of his beloved, Katia. And she was *his*. Half of her very being was made up from Loki's DNA. Tom, Loki's identical twin brother, was Gaia's biological father. But that made no difference. The DNA was the same. Gaia belonged to him in every way that mattered.

And soon they would be together twenty-four hours a day, seven days a week. Loki would never be lonely again. He was also sure that with time, Gaia would thank him for what he planned to do. Yes. He was positive, in fact.

But the horrible
truth was, Mike
hadn't been
responsible
for the
poison that **heroin**
had entered **chic**
his bloodstream.
He had been a
victim of Ella
Niven.

One Little Thing

SAM MOON CURSED SILENTLY UNDER his breath as he dropped a quarter into the phone's coin slot. It figured that class would let out fifteen minutes late when he had to meet Gaia. Students jostled him, hurrying out the door and into the cold night. She would wait for him, though, wouldn't she? Yeah. Of course she would. He just had to take care of one little thing first.

He punched the number into the keypad. It hadn't taken him long to memorize it. After calling the hospital several times daily to check on Mike Suarez's condition, the number was as firmly ingrained in his mind as his own birthday.

Once again, as the phone rang on the other end, Sam's head swam with the horrible images of finding Mike unconscious on the tattered, stained university-issued couch in the common area of their suite. Every time he called, it was always the same. It was torture. He'd assumed that Mike had drunk himself into a stupor at a keg party the night before. Then he'd seen the needle sticking out of Mike's arm. The rest was a blur: the paramedics, the drive to the hospital . . . the confirmation of his worst fear: Mike had overdosed on heroin, and he was in a coma.

But that wasn't even the worst of it. Sam could have handled that. He could have handled the possibility that Mike had just done something tremendously idiotic in a weak moment and would never do it again. But the horrible truth was, Mike *hadn't* been responsible for the poison that had entered his bloodstream. He had been a victim of Ella Niven. *Another* victim. A casualty of a psychopath.

But at least that witch couldn't harm anyone anymore—

"Fifth-floor nurses' desk," a familiar voice answered.

"Is this Michelle?" Sam asked. He knew most of the nurses by now. He was also aware that he'd managed to endear himself to them. Which was good. They were the ones who knew everything there was to know.

"Yes," she answered. "Who's this?"

"It's Sam. Sam Moon."

"Oh . . . hi, Sam." Immediately her tone softened. She sounded cheerful. That had to be a good sign. "I was starting to think I wasn't going to hear from you today."

"How is he? Is there news?"

There was no reply. On the other end of the phone Sam could hear Michelle breathing. He knew she wasn't supposed to give out information regarding a patient's condition over the phone.

"Please, Michelle," he coaxed. "I need to know."

She sighed. "Well, let's just say that your friend is out of the woods," she said finally. "We think he's going to make it."

Thank God. Thank God. Thank . . .

Sam bit his lip to keep from crying. Relief spread in warm waves through his body. He took a deep breath. "Is there any . . . permanent brain damage?" he asked.

Another pause. "It's too soon to say—but no. The doctors don't think so."

"Thank you, Michelle," Sam managed, his voice shaking. He hadn't even allowed himself to hope for news this good. "Thank you so much. . . ."

"You didn't hear this from me, Sam," she told him.

"No. Of course not. Bye, Michelle." He hung up the pay phone and sprinted out of the building.

Sam's lips trembled as he ran. Mike was going to be okay. He would heal, and then he would return to school and finish the semester. And no one would ever have to know what really happened. Sam wouldn't have to tell Gaia the truth. She had suffered enough because of his fling with Ella. There was no need to burden her with this new piece of information. It didn't matter now. Mike was going to pull through.

Sam picked up his pace, whistling under his breath. Finally his life was falling into place. In less than five minutes he would arrive at his dorm. When he got there, Gaia would be waiting. And for the first time *ever* they would be able to hang out without a kidnapping, mugging, or murder getting in the way of their good time. He could already feel Gaia's long, silky blond hair tickling his face. He could see the creamy skin of her cheek. . . .

He knew he was grinning like Howdy Doody, but he didn't care. He could think whatever sappy thoughts he wanted. He made a mental note to look up the word *bliss* in the dictionary. He was fairly sure that Gaia Moore would be part of the definition.

THE CABDRIVER KEPT GLANCING IN

his rearview mirror. And Heather Gannis's glare kept meeting him there. God, was he annoying. Why did he have to stare at Phoebe? Hadn't he ever seen an extremely thin, extremely pale girl before? This was Manhattan,

A Private Matter

for Christ's sake. Pale, skinny women lined the sidewalks from Wall Street to Harlem. Everyone looked like a waif. There was even a fashion term for it: "Heroin Chic." Lame term. Then again, it was a lame look, too. There was nothing glamorous about drugging yourself to death—or in Phoebe's case, starving yourself.

With one arm around Phoebe's bony back, Heather leaned forward and rapped on the bullet-proof plastic shield that separated the driver from the backseat. "Can you turn that music *down?*" she yelled. "I'm getting a migraine." She never understood why all cabdrivers insisted on blasting strange, Eastern-sounding music at top volume. It was as if they didn't *want* to get tipped. The driver stared blankly into the mirror yet again, but he turned down the music to an almost acceptable level.

"Heather, chill out," Phoebe said, smiling weakly. "We're almost there."

Heather frowned. But then she forced a grin. "Hey, the passenger bill of rights states that I'm entitled to a noise-free ride," she stated, pointing at the sign bolted to the back of the driver's Naugahyde seat.

Phoebe shrugged. She closed her eyes and leaned back her head. "Whatever. Wake me up when it's time to get out," she murmured.

"I will." Heather swallowed, staring at her older sister's ashen face. She couldn't help it. After a couple of weeks in the hospital Phoebe still had the aura of a concentration camp prisoner. The anorexia had taken a major, major physical toll. Despite the electrolyte IV drips, the protein shakes, and the vitamins, Phoebe's hair was still unnaturally thin and stringy, and her skin looked too big for her bones.

But she's making progress, Heather reminded herself. Yes. The doctors had finally determined that Phoebe was strong enough to transfer from the hospital to some kind of glorified halfway house in Chelsea, where a team of shrinks would try to figure out why Phoebe had become so obsessed with weight the minute she got to college.

"Don't you want to look out the window?" Heather asked, uncomfortable with the silence. "There are some seriously hot guys roaming the streets this afternoon. And I think I just had a John Stamos sighting."

Phoebe's eyes opened, and she smiled again. "No, thanks." She drew in her breath, hesitating. "Hey, thanks for coming with me, Heather. I don't think I could have dealt with Mom—"

"It's no problem," Heather interrupted awkwardly. She didn't want to get into any deep family talks right now. This was stressful enough. Besides, Heather knew exactly what Phoebe was talking about: their mom had a tendency to be overly cheery in tense situations. It was the kind of thing that made a person commit involuntary manslaughter.

Without warning, the cab careened to the other side of the road, narrowly missing a double-decker bus filled with badly dressed tourists. Heather flinched, but the sudden maneuver got her attention. They were almost there. *Girl survives eating disorder only to get killed in bloody traffic accident,* she thought angrily.

"Right side or left side?" the cabdriver yelled.

"Right side, about two-thirds up the block," Heather told him.

"I think I'm going to throw up," Phoebe commented.

"With or without sticking your finger down your throat?" Heather joked. *Oops,* she thought. Maybe that was a little too harsh. Whatever. She was the anti-Mom. No one had ever accused *her* of being overly cheerful.

"That's funny." Phoebe groaned. She sounded relatively calm, but Heather could see her sister's eyes grow wider as they neared the halfway house. Not that Heather could blame her for being apprehensive. Up until this point Phoebe's condition had been more or less a private matter. Now she was going to have to spill her guts (so to speak) with a group of strangers. Heather shuddered at the thought. She would never allow herself to get into a situation like this. She would never reveal her dark, dirty secrets—so that they could be dissected, analyzed, and debated. Even her closest girlfriends had no idea what Heather's life was *really* like. And that was exactly how she wanted it.

"This is it!" Heather yelled, spotting the address 1513 on an elegant brownstone.

He slammed on the brakes. The cab lurched to a stop. Heather's head nearly slammed into the partition. The meter read $9.40. Heather pulled out a crumpled ten-dollar bill and handed it to him. Sixty cents was *more* than enough tip for this jerk.

As Phoebe got out of the passenger side of the taxi, Heather grabbed her sister's duffel bag and slid out of her own side. She had barely shut the door before the driver screeched away.

Heather's eyes wandered up the front steps. There was no sign on the halfway house. It looked like any other Chelsea brownstone.

Phoebe groaned again. "I don't get why I have to stay here. I want to go home. Or back to school."

Heather glowered at her. "You have to stay here because left on your own, you'll eat half a carrot and call it breakfast, lunch, and dinner. Remember?"

Before Phoebe could respond, the front door opened. A plain-looking woman stepped outside. Her gaze instantly zeroed in on Phoebe. "You must be Phoebe Gannis," she called. "Welcome."

Heather gently took Phoebe's arm with her free hand and helped her up the steps into the warm and softly lit front hall. Maybe this place was a bummer, but at least it was a welcome relief from the cold, harsh hospital. Instantly it felt like a real *home*—clean and cozy and furnished with antique rugs. Heather allowed herself a sigh of relief.

"I'm Mariah," the woman said, closing the door behind them.

"Heather Gannis. Phoebe's younger sister," Heather replied. She shook Mariah's hand. She couldn't help but notice that the woman had the kind of all-knowing, unflappable attitude that Heather automatically associated with psychiatrists. It was kind of annoying. Phoebe hadn't even stepped in the door, and she was already under the microscope.

Mariah glanced at the bag in Heather's left hand. "Phoebe can carry her own luggage, Heather," she announced. "Part of the purpose of her stay here is to gain personal independence."

"Fine with me," Phoebe snapped.

She grabbed the bag from Heather. Her arm was so skinny that it looked like the weight of the duffel might make it snap off. Mariah forced a strained smile.

Great start, guys, Heather thought grimly.

She followed Mariah and Phoebe down the hall to the staircase, trying to ignore how miserable and uncomfortable she felt. Better to focus on the house itself. She had received strict instructions from her mom to inspect the place. And she had to admit, it was gorgeous. High ceilings, hardwood floors, fresh flowers. It looked more like the home of a New York socialite than a holding bin for troubled girls. She could even smell something delicious . . . something like homemade pasta sauce simmering. At the very least, it didn't look like Phoebe was going to be bundled into a straitjacket and hustled off to a padded cell anytime soon.

Mariah paused at the bottom of the staircase and glanced at her watch. "Phoebe, I'll take you to your room to get settled. Then we'll meet up with the rest of the girls for group therapy in about half an hour. You won't meet with the nutritionist until tomorrow."

"Sounds like a packed schedule," Heather joked.

Mariah shrugged. Her smile faded. "We've got a nice balance of planned activities and free time. Each girl has time to paint or write in her journal or bake bread . . . or do whatever else she chooses."

Heather raised her eyebrows. Nice. *Very* nice. It sounded more or less like a spa for unnaturally thin people. She imagined Phoebe lounging on the sofa in the middle of the afternoon, leisurely sketching a bowl of fruit. It was almost funny. *Too bad Mom and Dad can't afford to send both of us here,* she thought. Aside from the psychobabble, Heather would have loved to hole up for a while and forget about the rest of her life.

From: smoon@alloymail.com
To: gaia13@alloymail.com
Time: 3:57 A.M.
Re: While you were sleeping

Gaia,

Did you know that you have a tendency to snore? It's not one of those chain-saw snores. Just a light, pleasant buzzing as you breathe. I know this because I'm listening. And I'm looking at you. In case you didn't know, you're beautiful when you're asleep. So beautiful that it was imperative I *tell* you. *Right now.* But I figured you might get cranky if I woke you up. I thought it would be best to log on and send an e-mail rather than risk your wrath by waking you up. Then again, if I woke you up, maybe we could . . . never mind. Isn't it illegal to transmit pornography via the Internet?

Good night, Sleeping Beauty.

From: gaia13@alloymail.com
To: shred@alloymail.com
Time: 7:45 A.M.
Re: Physics notes

Hey, Ed,

I would wait to talk to you at school, but things are . . . whatever. . . . I thought e-mail was a safer form of communication. Also, to be honest, I don't really know if I'll be going back there. To school, that is. I mean, I thought I would quit, and then I changed my mind, and then . . . never mind. Okay. By now you're thinking, who the hell is this person, and what has she done with Gaia Moore? To be honest: I don't know. Anyway, I just wanted to say what's up.

If you don't feel like actually speaking to me, a simple e-mail response will do. Okay. I'm going to check for new mail now. Who knows? Maybe there will be a message from you.

—The artist formerly known as Gaia Moore

To: heatherg@alloymail.com
From: shred@alloymail.com
Time: 12:45 P.M.
Re: Didn't see you at lunch

H.:

Where were you? Not in the cafeteria. Not in the library. Not in the ladies's rooms. (Okay, I don't know that for a fact. I took it on faith when the numerous girls I asked assured me that was the case.) I know you're worried about everything, and that makes me worried about you. So that makes today a great big worry fest. Maybe we all need prescriptions for Prozac. Yes! Great idea!

Love,

Shred

She stared
back at him,
uncomprehending.
Her heart
began to
pound.
Maybe
this *was*
fear. . . .

the

whole

truth

IT FEELS LIKE SOMEONE'S ELBOW IS

Hockey— Mask Guy

in my ear, Gaia thought in the split second before she opened her eyes.

Gaia turned her head and found herself staring at Sam's sleeping face. A shadow of stubble covered his cheeks, and his lips were slightly parted. Gaia wanted to reach out and touch the strands of hair that fell over Sam's forehead. But she didn't want to wake him. She just wanted to soak it in—this moment, this place, this boy . . . everything. She nudged the comforter that covered her body and peered beneath it. She had on her nicest pair of underwear (no holes, elastic unbroken) and one of Sam's oversize white T-shirts.

A smile spread across her face. She'd deliberately chosen to wear her nicest underwear because she'd thought that Sam might see it. And he had.

Everything had gone according to plan last night. *Better* than according to plan. After she'd managed to peel herself off the pavement after beating the shit out of that couple, she'd staggered over to Sam's dorm to find him arriving at the same moment—looking happier than she'd ever seen him. And then he'd swept her into his arms, like the most perfectly scripted moment. . . .

Sighing, she brushed her fingers over her lips. They

47

were tender and felt a little swollen. How long had she and Sam lain awake last night, making out on his grimy, narrow, dorm-room bed? Hours? Days? Months? Of course, they hadn't been kissing the entire time. They had taken breaks to whisper to each other. About everything. About their life. About karma. About whether or not the hamburgers at Googie's were better than the hamburgers at Ozzie's. About their favorite episodes of *The Simpsons* . . .

Of course, there was one thing that they still *hadn't* talked about.

Uncle Oliver.

Then again, there was still nothing concrete to tell Sam. After all, up until a few months ago Gaia hadn't even known she *had* an uncle. The existence of her father's identical twin brother was just one more secret that her dad had kept from her while she was growing up. And then Oliver had appeared out of the proverbial thin air and saved Gaia's life in Washington Square Park one night.

But did he really want her to be part of his family? And what did he know of her father and of her mother's death? What did he *really* know? Because in some dark crevice of her psyche, she suspected that Oliver had the ultimate, incontrovertible evidence that her own father was responsible for her mom's murder—

Gaia shivered. *Not now,* she told herself. This wasn't the time to dwell. Not with Sam beside her in bed. Better to think about other things. Namely, the fact that she still hadn't lost her virginity. Okay—obviously, she didn't feel the same pressure that she had felt a while ago. But still, in a way . . . *hmmm.* She squirmed, unsure whether she wanted to giggle or frown. Maybe she *did* feel pressure. She had been determined to do the deed for months now—but up until ten hours ago Gaia hadn't even gotten to second base. And once things had become hot and heavy last night, Sam had pulled back. He'd said he wanted their first time together to be perfect. Planned. "Special."

How much more special could last night get?

On the other hand, if she was going to have sex, she should probably at least shave her legs beforehand.

Without thinking, she kissed Sam lightly on the lips.

"Mmmm . . . ," he moaned. "Good morning."

"Sorry to wake you up," she murmured.

He smiled, but his eyes remained closed. Just staring at him filled her with a thrilling combination of light-headedness, nausea, tingling, and melting. Was this what fear felt like? Maybe. Maybe people who loved horror movies experienced something like this when the hockey-mask guy popped out of the bushes, wielding a chain saw. Only this was all about pleasure. There was no fear involved.

"I had a great dream last night," Sam mumbled sleepily. He rolled over on his back and yawned. "You and I were in a Winnebago, and we were driving cross-country. And we went to Las Vegas. You really wanted to play the slots."

Gaia laughed. "You know me pretty well, Sam Moon," she whispered.

Suddenly he rolled over on his side, facing her. His eyes opened wide.

"Let's do it," he said.

She stared back at him, uncomprehending. Her heart began to pound. Maybe this *was* fear. Did he mean . . .

"What?" she forced herself to croak.

"Go to Vegas."

Almost instantly her muscles relaxed. But she couldn't help feeling mildly disappointed. "Oh," she murmured.

"Seriously." He propped himself up on one elbow. "Picture it. Picture *us*. Traveling across America together this summer. We could go to the Grand Canyon. Mount Rushmore. That museum where they have the world's biggest ball of twine. We could pool our funds and buy some decrepit old car with two hundred thousand miles on it, and we could just drive until the thing conked out somewhere west of Colorado—"

"Whoa, whoa," Gaia interrupted, giggling. "Slow

down there, champ. Do I get to do the driving? I've never been a very good passenger."

Sam laughed. "You behind the wheel? That could get dangerous."

"Okay. We'll take turns."

Getting into the fantasy, Gaia pictured the two of them camping on the side of highways and checking into seedy motels. No rapists or serial killers or hit men to deal with. Just the two of them, totally and completely free . . .

"Who knows? Maybe when we get back, we can get a place together," Sam continued. "I could ditch dorm life and we could move into a cheap one bedroom in the East Village."

Gaia looked up into Sam's eyes. She felt that nervous flutter in her gut again. "You *are* kidding about all of this . . . right?"

He shook his head. "Nope." There wasn't a trace of sarcasm or irony on his face. "So what do you say? You and me and a rat-infested apartment in Alphabet City? Then we could hustle chess games in Tomkins Square Park. The caliber of players isn't nearly as good as Washington Square. We could even use that chessboard I gave you."

"What chessboard?" she asked, so overwhelmed with emotion, she could barely follow him.

"The one I gave you for Christmas." Sam raised his eyebrows. "Remember? You sent me a really lame e-mail saying thanks for the gift, but—" He abruptly broke off.

Gaia stared at him. Either she was suffering from early-onset Alzheimer's, or there had been a major communication breakdown. But then it hit her: *Ella.* Right. She must have somehow interfered, stealing the gift and sending a bogus e-mail in Gaia's stead. Another pang of regret shot through Gaia. If only she and her foster mother had communicated earlier, a lot of torture and suffering could have been avoided. But part of Ella had always lived for inflicting pain. . . .

"Ella," Sam murmured, as if speaking for both of them. "I bet it's still somewhere in your house. But look—it doesn't matter. What you do think of what I'm telling you?"

"I love it," she responded without thinking. "It sounds . . . great."

And that was the best she could do. Gaia was shocked at herself. She had never lied. *Ever.* And even though she wasn't technically lying, for the first time—for the first time in her entire *life*—she wasn't telling the whole truth. Yes, living with Sam did sound great. It sounded perfect. Idyllic. Only . . . so did leaving New York City to live abroad with Oliver. She just couldn't tell Sam that—not now. For just a little while longer she wanted to keep up the illusion that her life could be simple. Besides, if history were any indication, reality would come crashing in at any moment.

Then she would deal with the truth. All of it.

The Rent

HEATHER COULDN'T MOVE. HER BARE feet seemed to be superglued to the cold patch of floor in front of her parents' closed bedroom. Even though her mom and dad were speaking in hushed tones, Heather could every word. And even if she *couldn't* hear them, she'd know what they were talking about.

Money. These days, it was always about money.

". . . paid the rent ten days late *last* month," Mom was hissing. "We have to get the money together on time, or else we're going to have a problem—"

"I'm working on it. I already put a call in to my sister."

Heather swallowed. Dad sounded desperate. His voice was high-pitched, whiny. Out of control. Totally unlike the way he presented himself to everyone. She heard her mother sigh deeply.

"If we start borrowing from them, we'll never stop. Isn't there a way to do this on our own?"

"Have you seen the latest set of bills from the hospital? Even after insurance, the fees are astronomical."

Heather pictured the bare, sterile hospital room. Phoebe could have stayed in a suite at the Four Seasons for less. And the group home was costing even more. Insurance had labeled Phoebe's extended therapy "elective" and refused to pay for a dime of it. Rage simmered in Heather's veins. How could people be so unfeeling?

"You need to find another job," Mom suddenly stated.

Heather stiffened. *Another job?* Why on earth would he have to do that? His current job might not pay the hospital bills, but they'd eventually manage—

"How? At my age I'll be lucky to find any job at all, much less one that pays a decent salary. Besides, I was fired. People don't like to hire people who were fired."

The yogurt Heather had eaten for breakfast started to congeal in her stomach. Laid off. Fired. There had to be some kind of mistake. Her dad had been fired. She hadn't even known. Of course not. Her parents hadn't told her. All at once she began to shake. Her throat tightened. She bit down on the inside of her cheek, focusing on the pain in order to keep any sound from escaping her lips.

The rage inside her began to grow. A series of nightmarish images flashed in front of her. She saw herself being thrown out of the apartment with nothing but a pair of Gap jeans and her favorite agnès B cashmere sweater. She saw herself begging for change while her parents huddled around a trash-can bonfire. And what about Phoebe? Well, one thing was for damn sure. Without enough money to buy food, her sister would finally get down to her "target" weight of something like fifty pounds—

Heather whirled and strode back to her room. Enough. Her family was like a freaking hurricane that was whipping her in a thousand different directions—and she couldn't do a thing to stop it. She was fed up with feeling so helpless. She'd never been good at that. No. She needed to be on top of things. And there was only one person who could make her feel that way.

Heather wanted to be in his arms as soon as possible.

THE MOMENT ED PROPELLED HIMSELF

Some Pithy, Oscar Wilde—Type Phrase

out of the lobby of his apartment building, he nearly wiped out. Heather was standing right at the bottom of the wheelchair ramp, her face half concealed by the hair that jutted out from under her navy blue cap. Normally the fact that a beautiful girl was loitering outside his home would indicate Ed's life had definitely taken a turn for the better. But Heather's sour expression dispelled any fantasies.

He grabbed the hand brake and jerked to a stop. "Hey, what's up?" he asked nervously. "Couldn't wait to see me, huh?"

Heather tried to smile. "Something like that," she whispered.

Uh-oh. Ed took a closer look at her face. Something was definitely wrong. This wasn't the usual, gorgeous, perfectly coifed Heather. She wasn't wearing any makeup. Her eyes were red and puffy—and not from the cold.

"Did something happen to Phoebe? Is she okay?"

"Yeah, yeah, she's fine," Heather assured him distractedly. " I mean, I installed her in a luxurious brownstone on Seventeenth Street last night."

Ed's eyes narrowed. "So what's up?"

"It's my dad." Her gaze met his, then fell to the sidewalk. "He . . . ah, he lost his job."

For a moment Ed just gaped at her. He knew he should say something. But he couldn't. This would have been an ideal moment for one of those grand gestures when a man sweeps the girl of his dreams into his arms and tells her not to worry about a thing. Unfortunately, thirty pounds of plastic and steel stood between him and said

56

grand gesture. He reached out and grabbed Heather's hand, hoping some brilliant witticism would pop into his mind, some pithy, Oscar Wilde–type phrase that would make everything fine. But all he finally managed was one lame word.

"Harsh."

Heather laughed flatly. "Yeah. Harsh."

"Look, Heather, this isn't the end of the world. Things will work out—"

"No, they *won't* work out, Ed. My entire family—not to mention my life—is falling apart around me. I don't even know if I'll be able to go to college. I'm serious." Her voice rose, but her eyes remained glued to the pavement. "I should probably quit school right now and get a job as a waitress at Hooters just to help pay the rent."

Ed opened his mouth—then realized that this wasn't the moment to point out that Heather didn't have what it took in the chest area to work at Hooters. There was nothing funny about the situation. Nothing at all.

"What?" she asked.

He shook his head. "Nothing. It's just . . . you'll get through this, Heather. You're one of the strongest people I know."

And she was. Aside from Gaia, Heather had more steel inside her than anyone Ed had ever met. He knew she wouldn't let her family's problems make her crumble. Just like he knew that as soon as they got to school, Heather would take off the ski cap, put on her makeup, and slip into the czarina persona she used to rule the school. No one would ever guess that she had started the day in tears.

"It's funny; I don't feel strong," Heather admitted. "That Prozac you mentioned is sounding better and better."

"Well, how about we hang out tonight?" he suggested. "I have a doctor's appointment this afternoon, but after that, I'm all yours."

She nodded, finally raising her eyes. "I'm glad you asked because I don't think I could handle meat loaf and microwave mashed potatoes with the parents tonight."

"Good." He reached out and gave her playful slap on the leg. "Let's go, Hooter."

Heather sighed. "Why can't some uncle just die and leave me a couple of million dollars?"

Ed shrugged as nonchalantly as he could manage. "Never say never. Sometimes money comes out of nowhere."

WHAT IS IT ABOUT HEATHER GANNIS that makes otherwise normal males act like lobotomy patients? Gaia wondered. It couldn't be that she devoted herself to the latest fashion trends with the same intensity that

Tibetan monks devoted themselves to a life of fasting and prayer. So what, then? Okay, she *was* good-looking . . . at least in that glossy, fake, *People* magazine way. And she knew how to make people feel very small. That was always good for social status. But were teenage guys really that shallow?

Well, yes. Clearly they were.

Gaia had strategically positioned herself in a classroom doorway so that she could watch Ed and Heather from a distance without being seen. Being at school was bad enough. Gaia didn't want to completely kill the aftereffects of her awesome night with Sam by setting herself up for an unpleasant encounter with Heather. But it looked like Heather was never going to leave. Didn't she have to reapply her lipstick or pluck a stray eyebrow hair? It was almost as if Heather *knew* Gaia was waiting to talk to Ed—and was purposely dawdling in order to irritate her.

It wasn't as if Gaia wanted Ed to be sad and lonely and never to get any action. Not at all. But why did he have to be in love with the one girl who had made Gaia's life at this lame school a living hell from day one? That was no exaggeration, either. The first time Gaia had met (to put it nicely) Heather, Gaia had accidentally spilled hot coffee all over one of Heather's precious designer

59

sweaters. And the big brown stain that formed on Heather's sweater became a metaphor for their relationship.

"Bye, Ed."

Finally. Gaia struggled not to retch. After one last sloppy kiss Heather left Ed's side. Gaia waited until she was halfway down the hall, then trotted over to Ed's side and fell in step beside his wheelchair.

"Hey," she said tentatively. She wasn't sure how he'd react to seeing her. Ed still hadn't responded to her e-mail. In the past he'd generally replied within the hour—if not the minute.

He glanced up. A surprised grin spread across his face. "Hey, yourself. It's the ghost of Christmas past. Where have *you* been?"

Gaia blinked. *Jeez, Ed—well, actually I've been running around having clandestine meetings with my uncle and fighting assassins, and I saw my foster mother get shot—but not until after we bonded in a totally inexplicable way . . . and oh, yeah, I also finally got together with Sam Moon, and now I might be leaving the country.*

She shrugged. "I've been busy."

"So I'd gathered." His brow grew furrowed. "You look different."

She hesitated. "How's that?"

"I don't know. You have that same look on your face you usually get when you're stuffing it with

60

doughnuts." He smirked. "Are you happy about something?"

She could feel herself starting to smile. "I guess you could say that."

He raised his eyebrows. "Ooh. Mysterious. Do tell."

For some strange reason, Gaia felt a surge of warmth spreading through her. It didn't make any sense. Yes, she was happy to be finally having a normal conversation with Ed . . . but still. It was no reason to throw a ticker-tape parade. But ever since she'd kissed Sam, she didn't seem to have control over her emotions anymore. Was this what being in love with somebody was about? Turning into a goofy mess? She had to get out of here.

"Listen, Ed, I really need to talk to you tonight," she said. "Can you meet me at Jimmy's Burgers?"

Ed shook his head. "No can do. I'm having dinner with . . ." He didn't finish.

Gaia frowned. He must have just remembered that Gaia's feelings for Heather basically matched the Montagues' feelings for the Capulets. Once again Heather Gannis stood between Gaia and a simple objective. Too bad Gaia had been taught not to use her combat skills on scrawny, porcelain-skinned brunettes.

"Whatever," she grumbled.

Ed's face darkened. "Are you mad?"

She shook her head. "No, it's just—"

"Good," he interrupted. " 'Cause it's not fair for you to expect me to rearrange my entire life in order to eat a burrito with you. In case you forgot, there have been plenty of times when you've blown me off."

Gaia swallowed. She couldn't argue with that. Then again, she'd always had reasonable excuses.

"I'll call you later," he muttered.

With that, he went on his way. Gaia watched him roll down the hall. Well. There it was. Spelled out in plain text. No gray area. Ed Fargo no longer had time for her. And that . . . hurt. It wasn't an emotion Gaia allowed herself to feel very often. It quickly translated into anger. She turned to the water fountain and slurped up a drink. Some of the water splashed on her face. The cool liquid felt good against her hot skin. There was really no reason for her to be here. Maybe she should just go back to Sam's dorm room.

"Hey, babe." The voice came from behind Gaia's left shoulder. "I haven't seen you in a while. Why have you been hiding from me?"

Very imaginative, Gaia thought dully. She turned and glared at the guy—and almost laughed. He was wearing a purple sweatshirt. He was also about forty pounds overweight. He looked like Barney the dinosaur on steroids. Someday the guy would end up as one of those construction workers who howled at women as they walked down the street. But now he was practicing on Gaia Moore. Big mistake.

"I'd like to take a drink out of you," he said in a throaty voice that made Gaia want to puke. *Interesting*, she thought. But she had a better idea. She took a step away from the fountain, then faked a knee toward the guy's groin.

"*Ahhh!*" he yelped, jumping back and covering his zipper with his hands.

A couple of kids passing in the hall laughed.

Gaia smiled to herself. She loved the little things.

Genetic mutation. It's all the rage right now, according to *Inside Edition.* But I don't think yuppy parents would be so eager to engineer their blond-haired, blue-eyed children if they really knew what they were messing with. I'm an example of what can happen when nature goes awry.

It's not a birth defect. At least not in the traditional sense. I was born without the ability to feel fear. I am *never* afraid. Let me put it this way: When other little girls would scream and run from frogs, I would pick up the frog and wonder how it was able to hop. When other kids had nightmares after they saw *The Shining* on late-night TV for the first time, I sat up thinking about Jack Nicholson's acting technique.

But those are just trivial examples. When a normal person runs from someone with a gun or a knife, I'm compelled to jump in and fight. This doesn't mean I'm

stupid. I have an acute sense of
danger, and I'm never rash.
Imagine a human-shaped computer
that happens to have all of the
vital organs as well as the ability to feel shame, hurt, loneliness, happiness, and wonder.

That's me, in a nutshell.

I can't say I'm sorry I was
born this way. I don't know any
other way to be. It doesn't matter
how many times I see fear on other
people's faces or in their eyes or
in their voices. I just don't know
what they're experiencing.

There are a million clichés
about fear. The only thing we
have to fear is fear itself. Face
your fears. Don't let your fear
get the better of you. Read any
self-help book, and the author's
premise always goes back to the
importance of overcoming fear.

None of that applies to me,
though. I've managed to screw up
my life all on my own.

His
announcement
was followed
by one of
Gaia's
least-
favorite
sounds in
the world:
the cocking
of a pistol.

**the
path
of
loki**

THE WINDOW WOULD PROBABLY BE

Strident, Male Voice

expensive to replace. It was stained glass, and Gaia remembered Ella saying that she'd had it shipped from Italy. But Gaia would send George money for it—if she ever had any.

There was no other way to get inside. She'd left her key in the bedroom last night because she'd honestly thought she would never come back. And she couldn't get in the way she came out. Climbing *down* from her window was one thing, but she didn't feel like shimmying up a drainpipe.

She slipped off her parka and wrapped it around her right hand. Quickly she glanced over each shoulder to make sure some Officer Friendly or "helpful" neighbor didn't happen to be walking by. The street was deserted. The sun was low in the western sky, casting long shadows down the block. Better get this over with. She took a deep breath and punched her fist through the long, narrow window beside the front door of the Nivens' brownstone.

The glass shattered, falling to the hardwood floor of the foyer. Without wasting a second Gaia pulled her hand out of her coat and reached through the hole, groping blindly until her fingers hit the dead-bolt lock. Bingo. It turned easily in her hand. She stood back and opened the door, then slipped inside.

Once again the empty, dusty house filled her with a odd sense of uneasiness. But feelings didn't matter. She would be out of here soon. She was here for one purpose and one purpose only. As soon as her mission was complete, she would be gone. For good this time. Besides, it was a fluke that she'd come back at all. If Sam hadn't mentioned that chessboard . . .

But ever since this morning she'd been obsessing over it. She *had* to find it. Finding it would be like an exorcism, a way of purging herself of all the idiotic mistakes they had both made, of all the obstacles they had faced.

She opened the door to the front hall closet, remembering she had once spotted a gift-wrapped box in there, tucked way in the back. She had noticed it one day when she was grabbing her coat. Of course, back then Gaia had never lingered in the front hall for fear of running into Ella. It hadn't occurred to her to wonder what was inside the box—nothing about her life had made her believe it might be for her.

The little bit of sunlight that penetrated the house barely reached the closet door. She peered into the shadowy darkness. There was a light around here somewhere. . . . She felt for the switch on the wall.

There. She flicked it. Nothing. She flicked it again. Still nothing. *Hmmm.* Maybe she should go find a flashlight. She bent down and brushed her hands over the shelves in the back until her fingers felt a piece of ribbon. Aha! The box was still—

"Move and you're dead."

The voice came out of nowhere. It was strident, male. Gaia didn't recognize it. But she knew the man meant what he'd said. His announcement was followed by one of Gaia's least-favorite sounds in the world: the cocking of a pistol.

ED WHEELED FROM ONE SIDE OF DR.

Favorite Four-Letter Word

Feldman's empty office to the other, then back again. The jerk always kept him waiting. And Ed hated these post-appointment rap sessions almost as much as he hated the appointments themselves. How many times had he sat in this office, dealing with same old bullshit? *"Yes, I'm okay, Dr. Feldman." "No, school is fine, Dr.*

Feldman." "*Whatever you say, Dr. Feldman.*" The first dozen times he'd considered launching himself out of the thirty-story window that overlooked the Upper East Side of Manhattan.

But eventually he got used to it. It was just another inconvenience that came with the chair. Like always having to pee sitting down. Like always having to use an elevator. Yeah, that was right about where these visits ranked: habitual elevator use. So now Ed was just bored and slightly irritated. He scanned the walls, looking for something new. He almost laughed. What—did he think that Dr. Feldman would go crazy and spray-paint his office with gang graffiti? Dr. Feldman's decor was exactly the same as it had been for the past two years. There were the requisite diplomas from Yale University and Harvard Medical School, an amateur golf trophy, and a miniature reproduction of Rodin's *The Thinker*. How cute.

But the worst were those photos of his family ski trips to Aspen on his desk. It actually sort of pissed Ed off. Most of Dr. Feldman's patients had some kind of massive spinal cord injury. Needless to say, pictures of Susie and Jimmy standing proudly on a mountain weren't exactly uplifting.

Finally, after what seemed like years, the office door opened.

"Hi, Ed," Dr. Feldman said. "Sorry for the wait."

"No problem," Ed lied. He had a sudden, vivid fantasy of jumping from his chair and smashing Dr. Feldman's pudgy, balding, bespectacled head with an ax. But he plastered a fake smile on his face and wheeled himself to the huge mahogany desk.

Dr. Feldman sat across from him. As always, he took a deep breath and removed his glasses. With them he bore a strong resemblance to Dave Thomas, the founder of Wendy's. Without them he looked like some sort of haggard frog.

Now for the fun part, Ed thought. He knew exactly what was coming. Word for word. The conversation was always the same. Dr. Feldman would inform him of the following:

1. Ed had lost more muscle mass in his legs.

2. Ed was adjusting remarkably well to life in a wheelchair.

3. Ed should never give up hope because advances were being made every day.

The last part was the part Ed loved most. Hope! Dr. Feldman's favorite four-letter word! But Ed couldn't blame him. Oh, no. Dr. Feldman had every right to talk about abstractions like "hope" because he could run home to his lovely wife, dance her off her feet, then go on a walking tour of Europe with his perfect, ambulatory kids. Who *wouldn't* be hopeful under such circumstances?

"How are you feeling, Ed?" Dr. Feldman asked.

"Look, I'm sorry—but could we just cut to the chase?" Ed answered as politely as he could. "I've got a dinner date."

Dr. Feldman forced an awkward laugh, then cleared his throat. "Well, okay. First of all, you've lost some more muscle mass in your legs. That's to be expected."

Ed blinked. "Really?" he answered, feigning surprise. "You're *kidding*."

"Uh . . . well—"

"And let me guess," Ed interrupted. His tone hardened. "You're *very* pleased with how well I've adjusted to life in a wheelchair. I'm an inspiration."

"Ed—"

"And finally, you'd like to tell me—"

"Listen to me, Ed," Dr. Feldman cut in. He leaned across the desk. Ed swallowed. For once in his life, Dr. Feldman's face wasn't a blank mask of phony sympathy and goodwill. His forehead was creased with concern. "There's something else I wanted to talk to you about this afternoon, Ed. Something very important."

Ed's pulse quickened. He stared at the man. "I'm waiting."

"First of all, I don't want you to get your hopes up," Dr. Feldman instructed.

Whoa. This *was* serious. This was definitely the very first time ever that Dr. Feldman had told him *not* to hope. And for some perverse reason, that only filled Ed with a nauseating excitement.

"There is a new, experimental laser surgery that's

being used on certain spinal cord injuries," Dr. Feldman continued. "Not everyone is a candidate. In fact, very *few* people are eligible for this surgery right now."

Something weird was happening to Ed's body; he felt like his mind had receded down a long, windy passage. He was watching Dr. Feldman from the other side of the Holland Tunnel. The words didn't seem to fully register. Experimental laser surgery . . . wasn't that the kind of thing they used so that people wouldn't have to wear glasses?

"I've gone over all of your records and studied your case in detail. I also took the liberty of discussing your case with a few of my colleagues."

Now Ed's heart was in full-on jackhammer mode. He didn't even think he could speak. "I see," he finally croaked.

"Ed, you're a perfect candidate for this surgery. I can't make any promises, but there's a possibility that we might be able to restore the use of your legs. I stress the word *possibility*. Do you understand?"

Okay. He'd heard wrong. Or he was dreaming. Or he was on some kind of wonderful acid trip. Yes. Someone must have spiked the lemonade dispenser in the school cafeteria. There was no other explanation. Miracles didn't happen. Not to Ed Fargo. Shit happened to Ed Fargo. Then again, he'd gotten back together with Heather. What the hell. Why *shouldn't* he be able to walk again?

"I'd like to talk to your parents about this. If you're up for it, of course."

Ed nodded. He was having trouble breathing. He had now gone so far down the tunnel that Dr. Feldman was just a speck of gray hair in the distance.

"Is this something you want to do?" Dr. Feldman was asking.

Is. It. Something. I. Want. To. Do.

"I think it is," Ed heard himself reply. "Uh . . . is that the right answer?"

GAIA FROZE—AS STILL AS ANY STATUE

she'd ever seen in a museum or an art book. Her training served her well. All of her senses were on high alert. Still, crouched on the floor with a gift in her hands and a gun pointed to her head, she was in a particularly vulnerable position. It was crazy. She had been close to death more times than she could count. So would her demise really come down to this? *Gaia Moore: shot in the head while searching through a closet for a missing chess set.*

Yellow-Bellied Lizard

74

"Don't shoot," she murmured. "Let me just—"

"Gaia?" The gun fell away from her temple.

Seizing the opportunity, she jumped and whirled around, still ready for combat. If necessary she could use the wrapped chessboard as a makeshift weapon. But then her eyes narrowed. Standing before her was the quivering form of her foster father, George Niven. Even in the darkness she could tell that he wasn't in very good shape. Bluish black circles ringed his eyes; his lined face glistened with sweat. His short gray hair was tousled, jutting in every direction.

"George?" She shook her head, bewildered. "Are you okay?"

"I . . . I . . ." He backed away from her and glanced down the hall. "Gaia, where's Ella? Did something happen to her?"

Suddenly it occurred to Gaia that George wasn't even supposed to be in the city. He had been out of the country on official CIA business, totally incommunicado. But how much did he know? And what was she supposed to tell him? *Hey, George, nice to see you. By the way, your wife revealed that she was a terrorist operative who only married you to get close to me. Oh, yeah—and she was murdered by a hit man that she'd actually hired to kill me. Wild, isn't it?*

"Where's Ella?" he repeated thickly. His voice was once again unrecognizable.

Gaia simply stared at him. She might not be able to

feel fear, but discomfort was absolutely no problem. "I—I actually have to go," she stammered, ducking the question. She glanced down at the present in her hands, then thrust it out at George as if to prove what she was saying. "I just came . . . for this."

George blinked, clearly not understanding her.

There was no point in prolonging this. Gaia couldn't break the news to him. Besides, he must have already known; he was simply looking for confirmation. She felt sorry for him, but he could hear the words from someone else. Without another word, she bolted from the closet and dashed down the front hall, throwing open the front door and clattering down the steps.

"Gaia!" George shrieked. "Gaia, come back here! Tell me what you know! Please. I have to know. . . ."

His voice faded, drowned by Gaia's pounding footsteps. She sprinted down Perry Street. She was a coward. A yellow-bellied lizard of a coward. But she couldn't stand to tell George that his world had crumbled. Grief, bonding, and comfort weren't her deal. They never had been. Neither had lying.

Besides, she felt enough affection and respect for him not to make up some lame excuse for the truth. She tried not to think about it—or the fact that she had just given foster daughters everywhere a bad name. But that didn't matter. She was no longer a foster daughter, anyway. She was a girlfriend and a niece.

TOM MOORE DIDN'T HEAL AS QUICKLY

Priority

as he once had. It was the price of age. He *was* relatively young, a few years over forty. But there was no denying it: He didn't have either the endurance or the recuperative powers of old. The shoulder wound was still tender, and it would be for weeks.

He winced as he sat up on the gurney and slipped his shirt over his arms. The pain wouldn't slow him down. He refused to succumb to it. But it *would* be a constant reminder that his life hung in the balance every single day. He glanced at the closed door of his hospital room. As if answering an unspoken prayer, it opened.

"The doctor will be with you in a moment," a nurse stated, poking her head inside. "He'll sign your release papers."

Tom nodded. "Thank you," he murmured. He watched the nurse as she crossed the room to check his chart. His heart stirred. There was something about her that reminded him of Katia . . . probably her dark hair and chocolate eyes.

He swallowed. There were moments when he could conjure his late wife in his mind so clearly that he could smell her perfume and taste her lips. But he had to ignore those feelings. They interfered with his objective. If he let emotion and anger cloud his decision making, he would go the path of Loki. He would let darkness and evil rule his life. None of Loki's sick obsessions would ever control Tom. . . .

He tore his eyes from the nurse and stared down at the cold tile floor. He had to get out of this place. He had to protect Gaia from whatever atrocity Loki had in store. The bullet wound to his shoulder had kept him out of commission for long enough.

"Stay safe," the nurse said as she turned to leave the room.

Tom nodded gravely. "I will."

The moment she left, a doctor in a lab coat appeared—one Tom hadn't seen before. He was short and thin, like all his other doctors. Pale, too. They all looked vaguely like moles. But in a way, that made sense. This facility was several floors underground.

"I'm getting out of here today," Tom announced before the man could speak. It was a statement, not a question.

The doctor nodded. "Don't worry. I'm releasing you. But you have to rest—"

"I understand," Tom interrupted, but his tone was soft.

The doctor managed a half smile. "Your wound has healed relatively quickly. But I'm worried about your blood pressure. It's getting up there."

Tom bit his lip. As much as he wanted to ignore the warning, he knew he had to be careful. His dropping dead wouldn't do Gaia any good. He took a bottle of blood pressure medication from the doctor as he slipped off the gurney. *One pill. Twice daily.*

"Be careful out there, Tom. I mean it."

"I will," Tom murmured. He didn't *feel* very bad. In fact, he felt heathy. It was good to stand. He'd been sedentary for far too long. He shoved the pills into his pocket, then extended a hand toward the doctor. But the cell phone in his other pocket rang before the man could shake it.

The two exchanged an understanding smile.

"Duty calls—if you'll excuse me," Tom said.

The doctor left the room without a word, closing the door behind him.

Tom pushed the talk button on his cell phone. "Yes."

"How are you feeling, Tom?" The voice was familiar. Tom wasn't surprised the call was coming now. The higher-ups had probably known the instant his release form had been signed.

"I'm fine." Tom knew better than to request a few more days off. Agents didn't ask favors—they obeyed orders.

"Good. You'll prepare to leave the country. Something has developed—something of a very serious nature. We can't discuss it any further at this time."

"Yes, sir." For the first time in his career Tom felt like making an obscene gesture at the telephone. Only the fact that he was positive a dozen hidden cameras were watching his every move kept him from doing so. These people had no compassion. No core of understanding. Tom had served his country for over thirty years. He was at the top of his field. He was "Enigma," the world's leading antiterrorist operative. He had sacrificed everything for them. His family. His *life*. His daughter was in danger, and Loki was going to—

"This situation is going to require your full attention. You do understand that?"

Tom's jaw tightened. "Yes, sir."

"You have been shirking your duties for months now, Tom. Don't let us down again."

There was a click, and the line went dead. Strangely he felt no fear, even though his life had plainly been threatened. He was beyond fear. He'd accomplish their mission, whatever it was. But his priority was Gaia. Always Gaia.

AN IV BAG DRIPPED CLEAR LIQUID

into Mike's veins, and a heart monitor beeped ominously beside the bed. Even from his stance at the door Sam could see that the guy had lost close to ten pounds in the last few days. How could he be out

Sick Bastard

of the woods? His skin was the color of ash. It wasn't until Mike's eyelids fluttered open that Sam was convinced his friend was even alive.

"Hey, Moon," Mike croaked. His voice was like sandpaper. "What's shakin'?"

Sam tried to smile. "Must have been one hell of a party, Suarez."

"Yeah." He grinned ruefully. "I guess I've got the mother of all hangovers to prove it, huh?"

"Right." For some reason, Sam couldn't bring himself to make eye contact. Of course, maybe that was because he knew that *he* was the one who had put Mike here. Or maybe it was because he secretly hoped that Mike wouldn't remember anything. Maybe it was because Sam prayed that Mike believed he'd tried heroin in a drug- and alcohol-induced frenzy. Because then . . . well, then Sam Moon would be off the hook.

He sauntered across the room and sat down in the chair next to Mike's bed, keeping his head down the whole time. "So. Do you, uh, remember anything that happened?"

Mike sniffed. "Nah. I mean, I don't know. Sort of. I was at a party most of the night. I chugged like two quarts of beer."

Sam nodded. His eyes remained pinned to his folded hands, resting in his lap. There was nothing unusual about that. Mike had been consuming massive amounts of alcohol all semester. And if his memory was foggy, chances were good he could have had a blackout. Chances were good he could have done *anything*.

"And then what?"

Several seconds passed before Mike even breathed. "I don't know, man." His voice quavered. "That's the scary thing. I mean, I don't remember doing the heroin. I've done a lot of messed-up shit in my life, but that stuff is way beyond anything I've even considered trying."

"But it was in your system," Sam heard himself say. "So you must have decided to try it. Maybe you just don't remember because of what happened afterward." A sickening icy sensation tore through his stomach. For Christ's sake . . . who *was* he right now? What kind of sick bastard would try to manipulate his friend's memory to save his own skin? To convince somebody that he had almost killed himself?

The kind of sick bastard who wants to hold on to what he's got, a silent voice answered. It was true. Sam might be a sniveling wimp, but he'd never had more to lose. Gaia was finally his. He couldn't afford to risk—

All at once he realized his knee was jiggling nervously. He clamped his hand around his knee to stop it.

"You all right, man?" Mike asked.

Sam nodded vigorously. Talk about sick: The guy in the bed was asking *him* if *he* was all right. "Yeah . . .

it's just—I don't know. Hospitals make me nervous."

"Tell me about it." Mike chuckled, then squirmed in his sheets. "Try talking to *cops* in a hospital. It'll do wonders for low blood pressure—"

"Wait, did you say cops?" Sam interrupted. His head jerked up. His heart immediately snapped into overdrive. "What did they want?"

"Who knows?" Mike's eyelids were drooping. He yawned. "It was some detective guy. Pantis. Mantis. Something like that."

Sam leaned over Mike's bed, struggling to remain calm. "Are they going to press charges against you? Is that why he was here?"

Mike shook his head. "Nah . . . they just needed to ask me some questions. Kind of a routine thing." His eyes closed all the way.

Damn it. Sam wanted to grill Mike some more, but it was useless. The guy was already half asleep. Sam knew he should just get out of here. Especially if cops were snooping around. He stood up and clasped Mike's hand for a moment. "Take care, man. We're all pulling for you."

With what looked like a major effort, Mike opened his eyes again. "Thanks, Sam. You know . . . I, uh—well, cheesy shit isn't my specialty, but you're a great friend. I mean it. The nurses told me you've been calling and coming around every day. That means a lot to me, you know?"

Sam couldn't bear to look at him. He withdrew his hand. *Yeah, I'm a great friend, all right,* he thought, nauseated. *I almost got you killed.* He should have told the police what he knew about Ella right away. But it was too late. And if that detective went digging any further, he might discover that Mike hadn't stuck that needle into his arm. Then there were going to be a lot of questions. Questions Sam didn't want to answer.

When I was five years old, my mother told me about the meaning of Christmas. She told me about Mary and Joseph and the manger and the baby Jesus. I thought being born in a manger sounded like fun, what with the horses and all, but my mom pointed out that it must have been hard on Mary.

My favorite part of the story was when the Three Wise Men came. It was amazing to me that they could be guided to one little baby by a single star in the sky.

Of course, I didn't get what myrrh was. I still don't.

Anyway, I guess Mom wanted me to know that Christmas was supposed to be about more than trees and stockings and parents shoving each other in the aisles of Toys "R" Us. It's really funny, too, because my mom was Jewish. But religion wasn't the point. The *story* was the point. And since my Dad wasn't Jewish and since we celebrated Christmas, she knew I

should have some understanding of
it. Some *real* understanding.
That's the kind of person she
was. Smart. Inclusive.
Empathetic.

Back then, I didn't know how
many Christmas Days I would spend
alone. I didn't know I should
cherish every string of popcorn
and piece of tinsel. Ironically,
when my mother died, Christmas
stopped for me.

But this year was different.
This year Sam Moon went out and
got me a gift that I'll treasure
forever. That makes this the
best—the only—Christmas I've
had in years. Peace on earth and
goodwill toward men. I feel all
of that.

So what if it's not December?
Nobody knows what day Jesus was
really born, anyway, right?

In the filtered light from the bridge's lamp, a blade glistened. A tingle shot through her veins. *I wanted this, didn't I?* she realized.

an

intimate

moment

NOBU WAS THE KIND OF RESTAURANT

that ended up in every "Best of Manhattan" article and cost more per meal than some families in third-world countries earned per year. But that was fine by Ed. That was the whole

Shameless Desire

point, actually. Since he and Heather had sat down, Ed had already spotted one of the stars of *Sex and the City* and Donald Trump's ex-wife (Marla or Ivana—he could never keep them straight).

Normally Ed would consider coming to a place like this a disgusting and mildly pathetic waste of money. But tonight he didn't care. Tonight was a celebration.

There was actually a possibility.

A *real* possibility. He'd been given a vision of a world where this bulky wheelchair would be a thing of the past, where he could sit across from his beautiful and brilliant bombshell of a girlfriend in a normal seat and lean over and plant his lips—

Okay, he knew he shouldn't get too excited. The chances were good, not great. But still, he could actually allow himself to use Dr. Feldman's favorite four-letter word. He could actually allow himself to . . . yes, ladies and gentlemen, drumroll, please: *hope*.

"So what's this all about, Ed, anyway?" Heather

asked, scanning the menu. She laughed. "I've been wanting to come here for ages. You know, I have to admit, I even told Megan and Ashley that I already *had* eaten at this place."

Ed laughed, too. It figured. Heather and her friends kept a running tally of who had gone where and who had bought what. The FOHs were beyond snobs. They managed to make something like choosing a dentist into a status competition. But Ed didn't care. He savored the moment. In a weird way, that was one of the things he loved about Heather: her shameless desire to be on top of the world. She was totally honest about herself. Besides, he hadn't seen her *this* happy in . . . well, in years.

"So what do you want to start with?" Ed asked, hoping she would have a better idea of how to order raw fish than he would. The fact of the matter was that he was in over his head. Sushi? Please. He could imagine how Gaia would react to this meal. She would *freak*. He smiled. If something had less than three hundred grams of fat and didn't come in a paper bag, she wouldn't even touch it—

"What's so funny?"

Ed glanced up from the menu with a start. "Uh . . . n-nothing," he stammered. "I was just thinking that I have no idea what I'm doing. You're gonna have to order for me."

Heather burst out laughing.

Whew. *That* was lucky. Nice comeback there, Fargo. Most of it was true, anyway. Ed really didn't know what he was doing. In more ways than one. He glanced anxiously back at his menu. Why the hell was he thinking about Gaia? Tonight had nothing to with Gaia. He wasn't here for her. He was here for *him*. And for Heather. His grip tightened on the leatherbound menu. No more Gaia. No way. As of now, this evening would be totally Gaia-free. Gaia had no place—

"Let's just ask the waiter to recommend something," Heather suggested, putting down her menu. "If you want to know the truth, I don't know what I'm doing, either."

Ed managed a grin. He dropped the menu on the table and took a swig of water.

"So . . . you never answered my question," Heather murmured seductively, leaning across the table.

"What question?"

"What's this about?"

He drew in a deep breath. He was going to wait, to build up to it—but what the hell. He was never good at keeping secrets. "Well, I went to the doctor today," he began.

Heather groaned. "Oh, boy. I'm sorry, but can we not talk about doctors? Doctors make me think of medical bills, which make me think of the thousands of dollars my family owes to various institutions. And that makes me think . . ." She didn't finish.

Ed just stared at her. *That* sure wasn't the reaction he'd been expecting. But now he saw the truth: Heather was so caught up in her own problems that she didn't even see the connection between a celebratory dinner at an overpriced restaurant and the word *doctor*. Why *else* would Ed be celebrating? It sure as hell wasn't because he'd been elected to the National Honor Society. How could she be so blind? So self-involved? If Ed was talking about doctors, then he was obviously talking about his—

Wait a second.

No. She didn't see. Which meant something . . . something that suddenly made Ed feel almost as good as he'd felt in that doctor's office. Heather didn't automatically assume that *doctor* was to *Ed* as *cure* was to *paralysis*. And that meant she no longer saw the wheelchair. She only saw Ed. Well, she *did* see the wheelchair—but only in the same way she saw Ed's ridiculous outfit: the dark suit and tie he'd been forced to put on in order to eat at this place. The point was, she mostly saw *him*. The guy. Not the condition. It was a breakthrough. A *huge* breakthrough.

". . . walk around school the way I always did, but the fact is that I might be homeless next month."

Ed hadn't even realized she was talking. Instinctively he reached across the table and took her hand. "Heather, you're not going to be homeless," he said, soothing.

She flashed a brittle smile. "I know. I'm sorry. I'm rambling. But look, can we go by Scores after dinner? I hear those strippers make, like, five hundred bucks a night."

Ed laughed. "You're going to dance on a greasy pole? I don't think so."

"Okay, then. I'll be a sex phone operator."

"I don't know," Ed mumbled jokingly. "Let's hear your audition. I'll judge whether or not you'll get hired."

Heather flipped her hair behind her shoulders and eyed Ed with a look of exaggerated sexiness. She slouched in her new red dress. "Hi, there, big boy," she whispered. "What are you wearing? Oh, nothing? Well, guess what; neither am I—"

"Stop!" Ed cried, holding up his hands. "You're making me sick. I mean, you know, in a really good way."

She giggled. "So I get the job?"

"Definitely. But I . . ." Ed stopped talking.

Tears were suddenly rolling down Heather's cheeks. But she was still laughing. Okay. Major problem. Rewind.

"Heather, what's wrong?"

"I . . ." She shook her head, biting her lip. "I'm sorry, Ed. I'm trying . . . really. But every time I have a second to *think,* I just can't. Everything is too screwed up. My parents are broke, Ed." Her voice caught. "And Phoebe . . ."

She wasn't laughing anymore. She was only crying.

Damn. He had known she was bummed out. But Ed had never seen the great Heather Gannis in despair. She had mastered the art of the emotional mask. Seeing her actual tears in public was the equivalent of spotting Elvis Presley, alive and well, in the middle of Times Square.

"I think now would be a good time to tell you that I won twenty-six million dollars in my lawsuit," he whispered. "As soon as the appeal is over."

She sniffed and looked at him. She didn't say a word, but her eyes flickered.

"Come on, Heather." His grip tightened on her hand. "I could never spend that much money. I promise I'll take care of you and your family until things get better. You are *not* going to be homeless."

Heather wiped her cheeks with her napkin. "I couldn't take your money—it would be wrong. I shouldn't be bawling on your shoulder, anyway. . . ."

Ed swallowed. "It's my money," he stated. "I can do what I want with it." Maybe tonight wasn't the right time to tell Heather about the operation. Besides, he had no idea whether or not it would be a success. Why build up her hopes? Right. He would keep the news to himself for now. It would be the best thing for everyone. For now, he would make Heather happy.

"I CAN'T BELIEVE I'VE NEVER DONE
this," Sam whispered, shivering. "It's amazing."

Walking across the Brooklyn Bridge had been Gaia's idea. It was one of her favorite New York activities, mainly because it didn't cost anything. Of course,

Less Than Nothing

she hadn't done it in a very long time, and not only because of the cold. Mostly she hadn't done it because she'd been mushed too deep inside her own trash compactor of a life to think about taking time do something *fun* . . . for fun's sake. But now—and very suddenly, it seemed—she had all the time in the world. It was as if she had abandoned her own existence and been reincarnated as a normal teenager.

Gaia's eyes roved over the deserted walkway. Thousands of cars crossed the bridge every day, but like all things New York, it was also designed for pedestrians. Gaia would miss that about the city if she left: its pedestrian-friendly vibe. Well, *if* Oliver ever got in touch with her. Somehow, with each hour that passed, that seemed less and less likely. Maybe he'd disappeared for good. Maybe she'd never see him again. . . .

But it didn't matter. She had Sam.

She swallowed, glancing over at him as he peered down at the rippling black water. His eyes were like a little child's, wide and awestruck, as he soaked in the dancing reflections of the city lights on the waves. From here the Manhattan skyline looked like an architect's scale models. She stood beside him, huddling against him for warmth.

"It's so nice up here," he whispered, his teeth chattering. His gaze shifted to one of the city's football-field-size sanitation barges, slowly drifting beneath them. "Ah, the fresh smell of rotting garbage," he joked.

Gaia slapped him playfully. She never gave a whole lot of thought to matters like romance—but she had to admit, even in the freezing cold, the night *was* undeniably romantic. For one, the bridge was almost deserted. Not many New Yorkers were insane enough to venture out at midnight in winter. The only other pedestrians she could see were two shadowy figures, approaching them from the Brooklyn side.

Sam stiffened beside her.

"What's wrong?" Gaia asked.

"Nothing," he murmured with a chuckle. But she couldn't help noticing that his eyes were glued to the approaching silhouettes. "So what do you say we head back? I don't feel like catching pneumonia."

Gaia opened her mouth to argue, then thought better of it. It *was* cold. And if Sam was nervous about those guys . . . well, he had every right to be. New York City was a dangerous place. More dangerous for some than others—namely, those who weren't experts in a variety of martial arts or perfect shots. And just because *she* was a freak of nature who couldn't feel fear, she had to learn to empathize with people who could. Especially since she was in love with one.

Yet part of her still wanted to lie in wait like a predator—a predator who washed the city clean of scumbags who even *considered* messing with a young couple on a bridge, enjoying an intimate moment—

"Gaia, let's get the hell out of here," Sam hissed. His voice was hushed, urgent. He tugged on the sleeve of her parka.

The wooden walkway boards began to rumble beneath her feet. Gaia glanced up. The figures were no longer silhouettes; they were two plainly visible *guys*, running straight toward them. One of them was holding something. Gaia almost smiled.

In the filtered light from the bridge's lamp, a blade glistened.

A tingle shot through her veins. *I wanted this, didn't I?* she realized. Yes . . . deep in her subconscious she *wanted* to put herself at risk, with Sam at her side to witness it. She wasn't sure why. Maybe it was as simple as a desire to show off. Or maybe it was just because she wanted to prove him that she could take care of herself. No matter what the circumstances.

The guys were almost upon them now—not running anymore, just walking and smiling. Time slowed to a standstill. She was aware that Sam was tugging on her, yelling at her, but her mind was totally focused on the two attackers. One was about six-foot two, and Gaia estimated his weight at about 230 pounds. The other, the one with the knife, was shorter and wiry. Both wore ski caps.

"Hand it over, bitch," the taller one gasped.

Gaia almost laughed. Well, this guy wouldn't be winning any fitness awards. He was practically fighting to breathe. Did he even *think* he was threatening?

Sam positioned himself in front of her. It was sweet, brave (almost heart wrenching, actually), but foolish. He would just get in the way. As gently as she could, she pushed him aside and stepped forward.

"Hand what over?" she asked.

"Your wallet." The shorter guy waved his knife menacingly at Sam. "You too, asshole."

In a flash she launched herself into the air. She kicked, and her right foot came into contact with the blade. It flew out of the mugger's hand. He fell to one knee, clutching his wrist. "Shit!" he screamed. The knife clattered to the walkway, right by the fat guy's feet.

As soon as Gaia landed, the other guy pounced at Sam. But when the guy's fist came flying, Gaia gracefully darted forward and delivered a block with her forearm, using her own momentum to spin and deliver a punch to his mammoth gut.

"*Oomph.*" He doubled over, wheezing for breath.

The wiry guy's eyes flashed to the knife. He lunged for it, but Gaia kicked it as hard as she could, sending it flying through the railing and out over the water. It glittered for a moment like a falling star, then vanished from sight. Stunned, the guy froze. Gaia used the opportunity to seize his forearm, wrenching it behind his back. He winced, and his muscles tensed. With a shove she sent him sprawling by the feet of his fat friend.

"Get the hell out of here," Gaia ordered.

That was all the encouragement they needed. Clutching each other for support, they took off back toward Brooklyn, hobbling as fast as they could.

"Holy shit," Sam whispered.

But Gaia barely heard him The adrenaline was slipping away. Gaia clenched her jaw. That fight was nothing, less than nothing. But it didn't matter. She still saw the familiar black spots in front of her eyes . . . the way she always did before she was about to collapse.

"Sam, you're going to have to help me," she panted.

He surged forward. The next thing she knew, she'd slumped her weight against him. Instantly his arm encircled her waist.

"I've got you," he grunted. He half carried, half

dragged her back down the bridge, back toward Manhattan. From what felt like far away, Gaia heard his boots shuffling against the pavement. She knew she weighed a ton, but she was helpless. Asking her to walk on her own two feet would have been the same as asking her to carry an elephant on her back. But she was lucid enough to wonder: *Did I want this, too? Did I want Sam to see it—all of it? The skill and the weakness?*

"Are you okay? Should I call an ambulance?"

She managed to shake her head. "I'll be fine."

Slowly the world came back into focus. Gaia took a deep breath, pulling away from him.

"Gaia, we need to talk," he stated. His voice was cold, toneless.

She stared at him. "I . . . I know."

"Good." He took her arm and hurried her back toward the city streets. "Now, let's get the hell out of here."

Ugly History

IT WAS CLOSE TO TWO IN THE MORNING, but Sam wasn't tired. Far from it. The events of the night were still too close, too *vivid*. Sitting here in his dorm room with Gaia, chowing on Krispy Kreme doughnuts . . . he knew he should have felt content. But he didn't. He felt confused, uncertain. The fact of the matter was that he'd devoted a good chunk of the last five months to Gaia Moore, and he still knew almost nothing about her. Yes, they had a connection. Yes, they were attracted to each other. But it was all intangible. There was nothing *concrete*. In many ways—many important ways—Gaia was a complete stranger, more so now than ever. And it scared him.

"So . . . I don't get it," he murmured, staring at her as she lounged on his unmade bed. "You're a kung fu expert? Like Jackie Chan?"

Gaia smirked. "That's *Ms.* Jackie Chan to you."

Sam grinned, but he didn't know what to make of the reply. It was classic Gaia: smart, quick—and totally unrevealing.

"I'm a pretty good shot, too," she added, seemingly out of nowhere. "And I can hold my breath under water for about three minutes—on a bad day." She shot him a seductive glance. "Not to brag or anything."

"No, please," Sam mumbled. "Brag away." After all, if Gaia hadn't been on that bridge with him, there was a very good chance he'd be sliced to ribbons right now or lying on the bottom of the East River. He didn't know whether to feel ashamed or relieved. Sam had thought he was involved with a girl. But Gaia was more like a superhero, like a comic-book character. (Okay, a very sexy one.) Or was she a super*villain?* He still couldn't tell.

He just knew that he was glad she was on *his* side.

"My dad taught me all that stuff," she muttered, grabbing another doughnut from the box. "He taught me how to be a fighting machine."

Sam looked at her closely. The muscles in her face had tightened. Her eyes seemed to change color, too . . . almost to a bluish black. Obviously there was some history between her and her father. Ugly history. It was bizarre even to think of Gaia in the context of *having* a father. Somehow Sam had assumed that she had sprung to life the first day he saw her in the park. He had never imagined her as a seven-year-old, learning how to ride a bike. Or in her case, learning how to catch a speeding bullet between her teeth.

"Why did he do it?" he prodded. "I mean, aren't little girls supposed to play with Barbie dolls and Easy-Bake ovens?"

Gaia laughed shortly. "I'm not really sure. My dad was a CIA agent—he probably still is. Maybe he thought I'd grow up to be one, too." She bit into the doughnut as if proclaiming that one's father was a spy was entirely routine. "Too bad I want to be a waitress," she added with her mouth full.

Sam chewed his lip. "Did he teach you to be brave, too?"

Gaia smiled wryly. "Nah . . . he didn't teach me that."

"So is your dad out on a mission now?" he asked, suddenly overcome with curiosity. "Is that why you've been living with George?"

"No." Gaia shook her head. "I mean, yeah, he might be on a mission, but that's not why I was living with . . . George."

Sam braced himself. He'd never heard this tone in Gaia's voice . . . this weakness. He'd heard anger, irritation, occasional happiness. But right now she just sounded defeated. "So why did you end up with George?" he pressed.

She tossed the rest of her doughnut back into the box and met his gaze. "My mother was murdered," she stated simply. "The night of her death my dad disappeared without a word. Just up and split. No note. No forwarding address."

"I . . ." Sam felt his throat constrict. The intensity of Gaia's stare made it clear:

She wasn't going to give up any details about her mother's death. And Sam wasn't about to ask. If he pushed too hard, Gaia would retreat. That he knew. But maybe if he let her tell him her story *her* way, eventually she would let him in on whatever secrets were locked up in that inscrutable past of hers.

"I can stand a lot, Sam," she added quietly. "But not pity."

He nodded. "So, you're all alone. No family anywhere?"

An unreadable expression flickered across her face. "Well . . . I have an uncle. My dad's brother. I met him a few months ago. Until then I didn't even know he existed."

Sam's brow grew furrowed. "Why didn't you tell me about him?"

"I don't know," she answered quickly—almost defensively. "No. I do know. I'm not used to feeling like . . . well, like part of an actual family." Her voice grew strained. "If he's at all like my dad, there's a good chance he might disappear. So I try to pretend like he doesn't exist most of the time. If he disappears, I don't want to miss him. You know what I'm saying?"

But I'm your family, Sam wanted to promise. *I'll never disappear.* This was a Gaia he had never seen before. `Even the night of Ella's death, she had been strong.` She had been a woman—no, more than that. But sitting on his bed, wearing one of Sam's huge sweatshirts and a pair of his boxers, she looked like a little girl.

"It's okay," he whispered, not even knowing why.

Gaia drew in a deep breath. "I miss my mom," she said.

Sam nodded. Without another word, he drew her into his arms. She rested against him, eyes closed, breathing evenly. That was enough family history for one night. Maybe somewhere down the road he'd learn a little more, bit by bit. When she was ready. But for now, it was plenty. They had the rest of their lives to get to know each other. He imagined their futures as two intertwined trees, climbing higher and higher, with branches stretching in every direction. Tonight was just the seed.

To: L
From: BFF
Date: February 2
File: 776244
Subject: George Niven
Last Seen: Washington Square Park

Update: Subject observed at known CIA safe house.
Intelligence indicates he learned the truth about
his wife. Uncertain whether he's had any contact
with G. Advise.

To: BFF
From: L
Date: February 2
File: 776244
Subject: George Niven

Directives: Forget about current subject. He's no
longer a threat. Find Tom Moore.

Twenty-six million dollars.

Let me just state that sum again. Or better yet, let me write it out. Just to see all the zeros.

$26,000,000.00.

Ahhh. There's a lot I could do with that kind of money. There's the apartment I would buy for my family. There's the health insurance, the flood insurance, the life insurance, the fire insurance, the whatever-ails-you insurance. There's the gas bill and the electric bill and the phone bill.

I could take care of all of those unpleasant facts of life and still have enough left over to go on a spending spree at Barneys New York every weekend. I could travel to Europe, go skiing in Aspen, sunbathe naked in the Caribbean. I could buy a PT Cruiser, a state-of-the-art laptop, an entertainment center, a yacht.

I could do all of those things
and still have enough left over
to pay my college tuition and
retire to Rio when I'm seventy-
five years old.

Of course, none of this matters. It's Ed I love. Not his
money, no matter how much there
is of it. I'm not going to let
him give me one, thin dime.

Well . . . not unless I truly
get desperate.

Sam Moon. He represents all things I despise about American teenagers. His clothes are sloppy. His hair is messy. He thinks with exactly one part of his anatomy.

And yet he thinks he's good enough for Gaia. Ha! The gall. He is a fool.

Not that he didn't serve his purpose. He came in quite handy, and quite by accident. Gaia needed a distraction while she got her bearings in New York, and he provided that. A necessary evil, one might say.

But he cost me more than the investment was worth. I think this boy must have too much time on his hands. Too much time to pursue Gaia—like a dog in heat. Too much time to allow himself to be seduced, as he did with Ella. That foolishness almost cost me years of careful planning.

In any event, the moment has come to deal with him, swiftly and decisively. Just so he knows that he has more important concerns than getting my niece into bed.

At that
moment Ed
literally
felt like

comforting

somebody

others

had

plunged a

machete

through his

chest.

GAIA WASN'T EXACTLY SURE WHAT

Strong Suit

had drawn her back to school, the scene of so many heinous episodes in her life. If there were any one place that perfectly represented everything she hated about her move to New York, this was it. But at the same time this school also represented something weirdly positive. It might be chock-full of morons and idiots and FOHs, but it was harmless. It was *safe*.

Besides, the truth of it was that she was bored. Sam had gone off to class, and that left her . . . well, alone.

As she climbed the steps, she wondered if the Village School would even want her *back*. After all, she'd ditched far more classes than she'd attended in the past few weeks. And in the brief time she *had* been here, she had threatened to break the leg of some beefy senior who had been picking on this poor little fat kid. What else? Oh, yeah, yesterday she told Mrs. Reingold, her calculus teacher, that her knowledge of math was on a par with one of Jane Goodall's gorillas. She stared down at the crumbling concrete stairs. It was kind of funny. She hadn't learned a single thing in this place—other than that most kids her age were assholes.

"Gaia?"

She glanced up. *Holy shit.*

"George?" she asked, incredulous. Once again he looked like hell. Gray whiskers covered his face, and it seemed like he had lost half of what was left of his hair in the past twelve hours. He was lurking in the shadows behind one of the big stone pillars that lined the front stoop, ducking the rush of kids. "What are you doing here?"

"Looking for you," he answered, eyeing the other students warily. "Listen, we need to talk, okay?"

"Yeah." Gaia swallowed. "Sure." She scrutinized his lined face. His eyes were rheumy, puffy—as if he'd been crying. He must have learned the truth. Of course. He was an agent. He must have learned everything by now. But what did that mean for *her*? She felt sorry for George, and she truly wanted him to be okay, but he was part of a past she had no intention of revisiting.

"Is there somewhere we can go?" he asked.

She shrugged. "Right here is as private a place as any."

He nodded. The last of the late-morning stragglers filed into the school building, and the doors slammed shut behind them. Gaia shivered, wrapping her arms around herself. She wasn't sure if she wanted to hear what he had to say.

"I know what happened," he began. "I know all of it."

110

It was a sweeping, yet ambiguous statement. But she understood.

He sighed, avoiding her gaze. "I never should have trusted Ella. I was foolish, and I'll pay for that foolishness for the rest of my life. But worst of all, I put you in harm's way—"

"That wasn't your fault," Gaia interrupted. "You did the best you could." The words were as flimsy and empty as an old gum wrapper, but Gaia could think of nothing else to say. Comforting others had never been her strong suit. "Anyway . . . Ella changed. She told me who she really was. She admitted everything. And she regretted the decisions she had made. She . . ." Gaia stopped. It was another stream of blather, utterly meaningless. Yes, it was true, but what difference did it really make? What she really wanted to say was this: *Get out of here, George. Leave this city. Forget you ever knew Ella, or Tom Moore, or me. Go someplace far away. . . .*

George shook his head. "It never should have come to that. . . . But look, it doesn't matter. I've got to think of the future now. I've got to salvage what's left." He raised his eyes. "I know you've moved all of your belongings out of the brownstone. Your room looks like you were never there."

A pang of guilt shot through her. She should have left a note. She should have done *something*.

She didn't want to hurt George—but now she saw that by doing nothing, she'd hurt him even more.

"Will you move back in?" he whispered. "Please? A girl your age needs a home. And I know I'm not much of a family, but I would love it if you'd let me try to be there for you. I owe it to your father. And myself."

She nodded. A painful lump was forming in her throat. George needed her. That was the message. She was all he had left. And regardless of what she felt for or knew of her father, George was innocent. He was a *victim*. Gaia had always prided herself on being there for the victims—for all the people who were manipulated and abused and beaten. George had been beaten in every way conceivable.

It won't be so bad, Gaia told herself. Now that Ella was gone, the Perry Street house would be very different. Sad, yes—but maybe peaceful, too. Besides, she couldn't stay with Sam forever. And Uncle Oliver still hadn't contacted her. Even if he *did*, what would she tell him? She didn't *want* to leave. Not yet. Not when she and Sam were finally connecting. Her uncle would understand. If he ever *did* contact her, they could get to know each other right here in New York City. For the time being, she would remain with George.

"Sure," she heard herself say. "I'll come home."

WHAT POSSESSED HIM TO GET *SOUP*

Overpaid Hollywood Hack

at lunch?

It didn't matter how skilled Ed was at maneuvering his wheelchair. There were certain items that weren't intended to be carried on one's lap. And hot vegetable soup was one of them. He watched as the broth sloshed out of the bowl and onto his ham sandwich. Wet bread. Moist ham. Yum, yum. Ed wasn't a soup kind of guy. And he sure as hell wasn't a wet sandwich kind of guy. So what was he thinking?

"Hey, Fargo."

Two long legs lurched in front of Ed. He stopped abruptly. More of the soup spilled. Great. It was looking like a perfect lunch period. Oh, yes. To make matters even better, the legs were attached to Carl Marino, one of Ed's least-favorite members of the Village School student body. And that was saying something, seeing as Ed hated over ninety-nine percent of the population. (Okay, *hate* was a strong word. *Intensely dislike* was more accurate.) Two members of Carl's ever present posse, Jason Franks and Joe Greenberg, were at his side. Ed intensely disliked them, too.

"Can't chat right now, guys," Ed said. "Sorry. My blood sugar level is low. I need to eat."

Carl's puttylike face registered no response. "That's funny, Fargo. Is that why you and Heather are back together? She likes comedians?"

Ed scowled. He didn't like the way this conversation had started—and he certainly didn't like where it was going: namely, into bad made-for-TV movie territory. He couldn't believe that guys like Carl actually existed in real life. They usually sprang from the mind of some overpaid Hollywood hack writer. So there was no point in continuing.

"She's hot, dude," Carl went on. "I know she had a thing for you way back when, but it's news that she's gotten into the whole . . . *vertically challenged* thing."

This time Ed almost laughed. Carl had been far too generous. Ed wasn't the comedian. *He* was. Maybe it was time to say something equally stupid in return.

"I guess she prefers vertically challenged to mentally challenged," Ed stated brightly.

"Can a crippled guy do it?" Joe asked. "Or does it, like, not work?"

Oh, no! Stop it! You're killing me! Ed smirked. They had great material, these guys. It just got better and better.

"From what I hear, I should be the one asking you that question, Joe," Ed said. "Aren't you taking Viagra?"

The guys looked at each other in obvious incomprehension. Three syllable words tended to have that effect on the Carl Mallone crew. They were like stun pellets.

Carl stepped even closer to Ed's wheelchair. "Excuse me? Did you—"

"Hi, Carl. What are you doing?"

Gaia. She appeared from behind the wheelchair. Ed rolled his eyes. For once in his life, he was *not* thrilled to see her. In fact, he was kind of pissed. Gaia to the rescue, yet again. He didn't need her this time. Hadn't she quit school? He hated that she thought he was vulnerable. Having a girl—even when that girl was Gaia—swoop in and save him from a group of guys whose combined IQ rivaled his pants size . . . well, it was beyond humiliating. His jaw tightened. That surgery had better work.

Carl stepped back. Clearly he was afraid. As well he should be.

"Later, Fargo," he growled, shooting a glare at Gaia. He stormed out of the cafeteria. Joe and the other ape followed him. Ed didn't even want to ask. Gaia had probably kicked Carl's ass on three separate occasions.

"How's it going, Ed?" she asked, grinning proudly.

He stared down at his soup-soaked lunch, suddenly in a very sour mood. "What do you *want*?" he muttered.

Gaia's grin faded. "Are you still mad at me?"

"Look, I just want to eat lunch, all right?" he

spat, glancing up at her. "So what is it? What's so important?"

She blinked, then shrugged. "I just wanted to tell you that I was thinking about moving away. That's all."

At that moment Ed literally felt like somebody had plunged a machete through his chest. He stopped breathing. His face went slack. She was . . .

"It's a long story . . . but the short of it is that I found out I have this uncle, and he was supposed to take me out of town for a couple of months. But I changed my mind. I'm going to stay right here."

There was no point in trying to follow what Gaia was saying. None at all. Ed experienced about a dozen emotions in the space of three seconds, and he had no idea what he was feeling. But he was sure that Gaia was staying. At least, he thought he was.

"So . . . you're not going anywhere?" he asked.

"Right," she said. "And you know, even though you *are* a rude little weasel, you had a lot to do with why I'm staying." She flashed him another blank smile, then quickly exited the cafeteria.

Ed stared at her retreating form. He felt like he'd just been in a car crash or run the marathon. He was drained. But pleased. Very pleased. It was almost as good as the time she told him she loved him after they had fallen down the stairs in the subway. Not "that way," obviously. But then, nothing was ever one particular "way" with them at all. Whatever way

Gaia chose to express her feelings was good enough for him. It always was.

ONE THING HEATHER HAD TO SAY

Arm Candy

about Gaia Moore: She gave whole new meaning to the term *casual attire*. If Heather walked around in baggy jeans and a gray sweatshirt, no would know she existed. But there was Gaia, strutting out the door while Ed looked at her as if she were Marilyn Monroe reincarnated.

Heather thought of the first time she had seen Sam talking to Gaia. He had looked like one of the Seven Dwarfs meeting Snow White for the first time. Dopey, if she remembered correctly. Not so coincidentally, that was about the time that Sam and Heather's relationship started on its collision course. *Ka-boom*. Over.

Then again, Ed wasn't Sam. Ed loved her. He *really* loved her. And unlike Sam, Ed *knew* Heather. She wasn't just a piece of arm candy who looked good on his arm at frat parties. Not that Sam had ever thought of her that way . . . but still. She and Ed were soul mates. Besides, Sam had

117

never bothered to use his money to take care of Heather and her family. No. Ed was different that way.

On the other hand, it wouldn't hurt to remind Ed that he was no longer Gaia's sole property. Or that he had better things to do than stare at Gaia's butt. Right. She strolled toward the table where Ed was sitting, aware that plenty of guys were watching.

"Hey, Ed." She leaned over and kissed him on the cheek.

"Oh! Hey!" He jumped a little, then laughed awkwardly. "I was just thinking about you!"

Heather cocked her eyebrow. "While looking at Gaia?" she asked.

Ed's face flushed. "No . . . no, she was—"

"Don't worry about it, Ed," she soothed. She patted him on the head. Point made. Ed was Heather's again. And he wasn't likely to forget it.

From: (undisclosed sender)
To: gaia13@alloymail.com
Re: Apologies
Time: 5:25 P.M.

My dearest Gaia,

I am very sorry I haven't contacted you in the past few days. Business has consumed me, and I haven't had any time to spare. But I am still very sincere about our plans abroad. I know this is short notice, but can you meet me for dinner tonight? Compagno's, eight-thirty. I expect to see you there.

All my love,

Oliver

I bought condoms once before. It was last fall, when I was determined to lose my virginity with Sam. Things didn't go exactly as I had planned. I went to his dorm room and found him having sex with Heather Gannis. The fact that she was his girl-friend at the time didn't make me feel any better. For that momentous occasion, I bought a pack of Trojan Magnas. Call me an optimist.

That first pack of condoms went the way of my stolen mes-senger bag. I hadn't bothered to replenish the supply until this afternoon. Not that I'd needed to. A girl with size-ten feet, zero social skills, and a wardrobe from *Platoon* doesn't generally need to worry about safe sex. Or any sex at all.

Now losing my virginity isn't a possibility. It's a certainty. I want to be fully prepared the next time Sam and I are ready to

do the act. So I bought ten pack-
ets, just to be safe.

I think the guy at the counter
thought I was a prostitute.
Either that or insane. I couldn't
tell which.

I have to say from the outset that I hate to buy condoms. I always feel like some kind of demented pervert when I slap them down on the counter to pay for them. My solution to this problem is to buy as many other items as possible at the same time. I always hope that my three pack of Lifestyles won't be noticeable amid the pile of soap, disposable razors, Bufferin, and toothpaste.

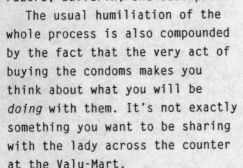

The usual humiliation of the whole process is also compounded by the fact that the very act of buying the condoms makes you think about what you will be *doing* with them. It's not exactly something you want to be sharing with the lady across the counter at the Valu-Mart.

I know Heather and I haven't been back together all that long. And I know I have a fear that borders on morbid at the idea of her seeing my pale, shrunken legs. But I think I could overcome that fear if at least I could stand up and walk to the bed.

The truth is that as much as I want to regain the use of my legs for a million reasons—skateboarding, running, surfing, driving, jumping jacks—there's one activity that stands out in my mind above all others. It doesn't take a brain surgeon to figure out what that activity is.

I decided that buying a pack of condoms would be a kind of self-fulfilling prophecy. If I *planned* for the operation to be a success, it *would* be a success. But believe me, a guy in a wheelchair hovering in front of a massive display of condoms is an awfully conspicuous sight. More than one woman gave me a dirty

look. As if it were illegal for a
handicapped guy to think about
sex.

But the best was the guy
behind the counter. His eyes
moved from me to the box of
Trojan condoms at least four
times before he finally rang them
up. I lingered an extra few seconds, just to see if he would
have the balls (like Carl's sweet
friend Joe) to ask if a guy in a
wheelchair could "do it."

He didn't, though.

"My girlfriend can't get
enough of me," I told him as he
handed me my change. "I just wish
she loved me for my mind."

The guy didn't laugh. People
like him never do.

The words didn't register. They floated straight past him. The sterile white hospital floor turned to **a curse** liquid. He pressed his hand against the wall for support.

LOKI HAD CALLED THE RESTAURANT

Supremely Delicate Moment

ahead of time to ensure that he and Gaia would have a private table—in the back, away from the Little Italy tourist crowd. He wanted her undivided attention. He *needed* it. And he was glad he had made the effort. Sitting in this small booth, across from his beloved Gaia, he felt that every other human being in this city ceased to exist.

Gaia was staring at the menu. He loved the way her long blond hair drooped around her face as she studied the names of the dishes. Her eyes were playful, happy. Of course. She'd been praying for this reunion. He could see it. She'd been thrilled he'd contacted her; she was even at the restaurant five minutes early, looking absolutely stunning in that same black dress she always wore.

"Do you know what you're having?" he murmured.

She shrugged and glanced up. "I think you're going to have to order for me again."

Loki smiled. "My pleasure."

She set down the menu, looking relieved. "Good. You know— " She broke off, her smile fading.

"What is it, dear?" He leaned forward, smoothing the lapels of his dark suit.

"I have to tell you something," she whispered. "Well . . . uh, I guess the best thing to do is to come out and say it. I've decided to stay in New York. At least for now." The words came tumbling out of her mouth in a rush. She nervously tucked a loose strand of hair behind her ear, then glanced up at him expectantly.

That's where you're wrong, Loki thought—but the expression on his face didn't change. He made sure of that. He was too well trained to display any disappointment or anger. In any event, there was no reason for anger. Gaia's statement was simply unacceptable. She would understand. No need to blow this out of proportion.

"Are you mad?" she asked.

Loki suppressed a smile. The girl was a wonder. Nothing escaped her. Nothing. He lifted his shoulders in a noncommittal fashion. "Just a little surprised. The last time we spoke, you were unhappy with your home life. What changed?"

Gaia sighed deeply. "It's complicated." She paused. "My foster mother is dead. She was murdered."

This was his cue. Loki made sure to look sympathetic. "That's terrible. I know you didn't get along . . . but it must have been an awful blow."

Gaia nodded. "I found out a lot about her before she died."

Instantly rage surged through him. Ella loved to talk,

didn't she? He should have shut her up long ago. But he didn't betray even the slightest displeasure. Instead he envisioned the look on her face had *he* been the one who had killed her—slowly squeezing the life out of her with his own two hands. He didn't make mistakes very often. But allowing Ella to live had been one of the biggest of his life. He wouldn't forget it.

"She wasn't who she said she was," Gaia continued. "She was only with George to get close to me."

Rage turned to fear. Loki's legs tensed. This was beyond unacceptable; this was dangerous. Gaia *couldn't* know the whole truth, unless . . . Was this a trap? No. She was happy to see him. Nobody could act being that sincere, not even Gaia. So Ella hadn't revealed *everything*.

"Why would she do that?" Loki asked, thankful that years of training kept his voice from trembling.

"She was working with my father. I don't know the details . . . but apparently my father is some kind of terrorist. He goes by another name. Loki." She fixed him with a penetrating stare. "Do you know anything about this?"

Loki summoned every ounce of concentration to meet his niece's gaze. So *that's* what happened. Maybe Ella hadn't been as useless and erratic as he'd previously imagined. Maybe she hadn't turned against him. In the final moments of her life she must have served him one last time. Yes. She'd convinced Gaia that Tom was Loki. It was brilliant. **Absolutely brilliant.** *Rest in peace, Ella.* Still, this was a supremely delicate moment—one that required perfect execution.

"I've never heard anything of the kind," he whispered. "Loki?"

Gaia nodded. "The Norse god of the underworld. It's fitting."

"I see," Loki said. Gaia's response was almost too delicious. The name *was* fitting, though not in any way that Gaia knew. But soon she'd understand the truth. Soon she'd embrace it. And as for now . . . well, he was safe. More than that, he had the advantage. The *ultimate* advantage. Gaia would never trust Tom again. She thought *Tom* was Loki. And that meant she belonged to Loki now—the *real* Loki.

"Anyway, the point is, George is a nice guy," Gaia said. "He's kind of old, and he's really broken up about Ella. I think he sort of needs someone around to keep an eye on him. I owe him that much."

Ah. He'd almost forgotten that Gaia was also full of compassion. An admirable quality, but one that didn't serve Loki's cause. He would have to find a way around it.

"Taking responsibility for a young girl might be too much for him to handle right now," he said.

Doubt clouded Gaia's eyes. Clearly she hadn't considered this angle. But then she shook her head. "George isn't the only reason I want to stay in New

York." She smiled, then blushed slightly. "I have . . . friends."

Loki nodded. Obviously she was referring to the Moon boy. It was ironic, in a way. He had wanted Gaia to make connections in New York City when she first arrived. It had been a way to ensure that she wouldn't run away in the dead of night and disappear from the radar screen. But those bonds had long since served their purpose. Now they were simply getting in the way. They had been for a while, actually. First there had been that horrible drug addict, Mary. She had made Gaia lazy, sloppy, out of control. But Loki couldn't dispense with Gaia's other friends' lives the way he had dispensed with Mary's. Gaia would get suspicious.

"Look, Oliver, I'm really sorry—"

"No," he interrupted with a smile, holding up his hands. "It's perfectly understandable. You have roots." He pressed his lips together. He knew that this game was drawing to a close; he had to make a decisive move. Fortunately, he always came prepared for the worst. He always had a dozen emergency scenarios worked out in his mind before he walked into any new situation. That way he was never surprised. Not even now. "Unfortunately, Gaia, I must go to Germany—with or without you."

Her face fell. "But why?"

He made a show of sighing deeply, as if he wanted

130

nothing more than for Gaia to roam the streets of New York with her pathetic little boyfriend. "My dear, I have been very selfish. The fact is that I haven't been honest with you." He paused, letting the anticipation build. "But I want to tell you the truth. All of it."

And when he was done, Loki had no doubt that Gaia would be packing her bags, just as he had planned.

SAM TUCKED THE STACK OF MAGAZINES

Screwed-up Friendship

he had under his jacket to protect them from the heavy, wet snow that had begun to fall. Maybe he was being overly optimistic to think that Mike would have the energy to read *Sports Illustrated*. But the practicality of gifts never mattered. People only cared about the act itself—the effort of giving.

Walking the last block to St. Vincent's, Sam prayed that this would be his last visit to the hospital. From here on out, life would be about studying, labs, exams—and of course, snuggling with Gaia under the new down comforter he planned to buy with the money his parents had given him for Christmas.

I won't stay for long, Sam decided as he pushed open the door to the lobby. There was no reason. Mike needed rest. Besides, Sam was in the clear— at least as far as any sort of legal responsibility for the overdose went. No one had called him in for questioning. Mike was right. The visit from the detective had been one of those routine paperwork things.

As he strolled into the elevator, he pulled the magazines out from under his jacket and pasted a bright smile on his face. Life could be extremely twisted sometimes. This whole thing had brought Mike and him closer together. And he was glad about that. Mike probably considered Sam to be his best friend. It was funny. Before now they had been suite mates, buddies—but nothing more. The relationship was pretty superficial. Yet thanks to a psychopath, a drug overdose, and a guilty conscience, Sam's existence was inextricably bound with Mike's. Were all friendships as screwed up?

The elevator door opened, and Sam strode toward Mike's room. The fourth floor was relatively empty. Good. The last time he had been here, Sam had seen a motorcycle accident victim being wheeled on a gurney. The guy had been moaning in pain and shouting about the foot that had been amputated in surgery. Maybe Sam didn't want to be a doctor after all.

"Sam?"

He turned around. "Michelle, hi." The pretty nurse was standing outside Mike's room, almost as if she were guarding it. "What's up?"

Her eyes were dark. "You can't go in there, Sam."

"Why? Are they doing more tests?" He tried to look through the window, but Michelle's body was in the way.

"I'm sorry, Sam." She sighed. "Mike died twenty minutes ago."

The words didn't register. They floated straight past him. The sterile white hospital floor turned to liquid. He pressed his hand against the wall for support.

"No, he was getting better. I just saw him—"

"The doctors did everything they could to bring him back, but the damage was too severe. He's gone." She stepped away from the door, giving Sam a view of Mike's body. He was lying on the hospital bed. His face was pale, and everything about him was absolutely still. The room wasn't empty, though. His parents leaned over him, silently weeping. Sam's stomach twisted.

"Would you like to speak to Mike's parents, Sam?" Michelle asked. Her voice seemed to be coming from another universe, another dimension. He was having trouble breathing. His heart seemed to stutter, then stop, then stutter again. "I'm sure that talking to one of their son's best friends would offer at least a small measure of comfort—"

"I need to go."

Sam sprinted toward the public bathroom. He reached the toilet just in time. Sobbing, he threw up everything in his stomach until there was nothing left but acrid, bitter bile. He could never look Mr. and Mrs. Suarez in the eyes, much less actually talk to them. He had killed their son, as plainly as if he had stuck the needle in Mike's arm himself.

GAIA WISHED SHE HAD ACCEPTED

Uncle Oliver's offer of a glass of red wine. She remembered how it had relaxed her. Not that she was particularly tense. Her mind was utterly blank—the same way it would have been had she been dropped into the middle of a demilitarized zone. Whenever her life took on some kind of cohesion, another trapdoor opened.

"I'm listening," she said. She wrapped her hand around her glass of ice water and focused on the condensation on the glass rather than Uncle Oliver's intense gaze.

"Five years ago I fought a battle with cancer,"

Oliver began softly. "I underwent surgery and chemotherapy. The disease went into remission. That's the good news."

Gaia just stared at him. Her pulse began to race. *Cancer.* It figured. Her uncle was dying. Everywhere she went, death stalked her. She was a curse. That was all there was to it. But . . . he looked so *healthy.*

He cleared his throat. "The bad news is that my doctors inform me that the cancer is back. It's in my pancreas this time, and the prognosis is quite bad."

As he was telling her this, she almost felt as though she could join in, word for word. Why would she have any chance at happiness? It didn't fit in with the scheme of the universe. Somewhere in the laws of time and space, there was a clause stating that Gaia Moore could never be truly content. It was one of those joke laws, like the ones in old town charters—the kind that stated it was illegal to gamble with ducks or that smoking a pipe was punishable by catapulting. Only the cosmic joke was on Gaia. Nobody else.

"They say I won't begin to feel real effects from the illness for several more weeks," he continued. He shook his head. "That's why I've been out of commission these past few days. I've been seeing doctors. They're all very pessimistic. I've had several opinions, and the consensus is always the same. They say that treatment would only prolong my life for a few weeks. But undergoing those measures will make me so sick that I won't be able to enjoy the days of health I do have left."

Gaia swallowed the huge, hard lump that had formed in her throat. She was not going to cry. That wasn't what her uncle needed. What he needed was *another* opinion. Maybe his doctors had gone to medical school in Granada or Belize or some other place that handed out medical licenses to anyone who could fork over the cash.

"I'm going to help you fight this thing," she heard herself saying, as if she were quoting a Lifetime drama. "We'll do it together." She blinked back that one stupid tear that kept threatening to slip down her cheek. "You can*not* give up hope."

He smiled. "Well . . . that's what I wanted to tell you. There's a place in Germany. It's a very small, very prestigious clinic where scientists are constantly experimenting with new forms of treatment for illnesses like mine. I'm going to go there and see what they can do for me."

Gaia fought back her excitement. So that explained why he would be going to Germany whether or not she came along. "And they'll be able to cure you there?" she blurted out.

Uncle Oliver shrugged. "I don't know."

Experimental treatment. Gaia knew something

about medicine. She knew that it could take years for some of these advances to be perfected. Her uncle was going to be a guinea pig.

"When were you going to tell me about all of this?" she asked.

"Soon. I just didn't know the words to use." He paused. "But I don't want this to change your mind about staying in New York, Gaia. I'm sure you'd rather be here with George and your friends than hanging around a sick old man while he tries to get better."

Gaia shook her head vehemently. She would not let him go the way of every other family member she'd had. He was *blood*.

"I'm coming with you," she promised. "I'll talk to George. I'm sure he'll understand the situation."

Her uncle frowned slightly. "No. This is a private matter. And even if your foster father agrees to let you go, we'll be bogged down in red tape with social services for so long that I'll be terribly sick by the time we can leave the country."

He was right. She had been a victim of the system for long enough to know that it took ages for the wheels to turn. If she did this, it was going to have to be on her own terms, without George's knowing until it was too late to stop her.

"Well, don't worry, Uncle Oliver," she assured him. "I'll work this out. You aren't going to do this alone. No way."

THE CHAMPAGNE WAS PREMATURE,

but Ed appreciated the gesture. Especially from his parents, who often gave new meaning to the term "socially retarded." But tonight they were doing all right. At the very least, they were doing a hell of a lot better than they did at Victoria's engagement party. He had actually been worried that their fake smiles would cause permanent facial damage.

All the Wrong Things

But that was the past. This was the present. And more important, neither his sister nor her lame-ass fiancé was in New York at the moment, so they weren't around to screw up the occasion. Ed lifted his glass at his parents. "Here's to hoping."

"This operation is going to be a success, sweetie," his mom replied, raising her own flute. "I feel it in my bones."

Ed rolled his eyes. Okay. Obviously they hadn't come *that* far. "Mom . . ."

"Now, come on, hon," Ed's dad said, clearing his throat. "Let's not set Ed up for a big disappointment."

Ah, Mom and Dad. Still with the knack for saying all the wrong things. What would Ed do without them? True, they provided hours of cost-free entertainment . . . but at what price? They present you with champagne, then bicker about whether or not the occasion is worthy of said champagne.

"Hey, the last time I came out of major surgery, I couldn't walk," Ed joked, hoping to end the conversation. "As long as I can still use my arms when I wake up, I'll be happy."

"That's the spirit," Mr. Fargo declared. "We'll just wait and see what happens. We'll take it one step at a time."

Right. Ed was quiet for a moment, waiting to see if his father felt compelled to spout any more clichés. When none were forthcoming, he decided to make his announcement.

"You know, if you don't mind, I'd like to keep the fact that I'm having the operation between us."

His mother raised her eyebrows. "What about Victoria?"

He shook his head. "I want to do this on my own, Mom. If there's a bunch of hype surrounding this thing, I'll feel like crap if it doesn't work. We'll tell Victoria when she gets back."

"I'm sure you'll want the support of your friends, Ed," Mr. Fargo added, chiming in with another adage. "If you don't—"

"This is the way I want it, Dad," Ed interrupted firmly.

His parents exchanged a quick glance.

"Um . . . of course," Mr. Fargo murmured. He took

a slug of champagne. "We'll honor your wishes. And you'll have your mom and me there every step of the way."

And we'll win one for the Gipper! Ed added silently. He almost felt bad for his father. The poor guy always resorted to the most insipid forms of bullshit when dealing with his kids. But hey, Ed should at least try to enjoy the moment. Things were relatively relaxed. It was a nice change. Since his conversation with Dr. Feldman, everything had been moving *way* too fast. Ed had figured that bureaucracy would hold up the operation for weeks, if not months. But Dr. Feldman was determined to go ahead as soon as possible. It was kind of fishy, in fact. Ed couldn't help but wonder if the guy was rushing just so he could become an overnight star in the medical community.

But whatever. That was fine by Ed. To use a cliché worthy of his dad, "the wheels were in motion." Ed would go into the hospital for a series of tests, pokings, and proddings tomorrow. Then he and his parents would fill out a stack of paperwork and sign a hundred different waivers.

Once all of that was done, Ed was good to go.

He grinned up at his parents as they silently sipped their champagne. It tasted syrupy sweet, like soda gone bad. People actually enjoyed this crap? But he wouldn't complain. He allowed his mind to wander, fantasizing about all the "what-ifs." What would his life be like if he could stand up and walk over to his stereo to put in a CD? Or hang a new poster on his wall? Better yet, what would it be like if he could get out of this chair, cross the room, and take Heather into his arms? He imagined picking her up and throwing her onto the bed. Ed would kneel over her, kissing her face, her neck. . . . He could almost feel her long blond hair tickling his cheeks as they kissed—

Blond?

Oops. Somewhere in the middle of his fantasy Heather had morphed into Gaia. And now that Gaia was in his head, he knew from past experience that there was no way she was getting out anytime soon. Oh, well. Nobody was perfect.

He only had to look at his parents to remember that.

THE SNOW WAS NOW FALLING SO

Code Name Enigma

heavily that Tom couldn't keep it from sticking to his eyelashes. He stepped farther back into the doorway of the building across the street from Compagno's.

There was little doubt in his mind about whom Gaia was meeting inside. Teenagers couldn't afford to eat at such a place—nor would they want to. But Loki loved gourmet food, and he loved to show off his wealth with expensive bottles of wine and lavish dinners.

Tom ignored his throbbing shoulder. His toes were so cold, they felt like they might snap off. But he wasn't leaving his post until he saw Gaia leave the restaurant. No matter what. Once again—for the fifth time in an hour—the cell phone in his pocket began to vibrate. *Damn.* He wanted to let it ring, but there was no point. His superiors would just keep calling back until he answered. He pulled the phone out of his pocket and clicked the talk button.

"Yes."

"Hello, Enigma."

Tom was surprised. He hadn't been addressed by his code name in quite some time. That meant the call was regarding a mission. It was probably coming from thousands of miles away, but thanks to technology, the voice sounded like it was just two feet away.

"Your orders have been issued," the voice stated.

"Yes, sir." Tom felt his chest tighten.

"You're to report to Paris immediately."

"I . . . I understand."

"Your contact will meet you tomorrow at six P.M. at

the hotel Belle Epoche. If you fail to report, we have advised the intelligence community that your employment is to be terminated."

The line went dead.

Tom thrust the phone back into his pocket, wishing he could smash it into the snow-covered cement. He wasn't in the least surprised. He had been sentenced to death by those to whom he had given everything—

Across the street the door to Compagno's opened. Tom froze, momentarily forgetting the call. There was Gaia. Loki was right behind her.

Tom watched as Loki hailed a cab for his daughter. *His* daughter! Not Loki's! He gnashed his teeth, resisting the urge to pull out his Glock semiautomatic and end his twin's life right then and there.

And then his brother gave Gaia a kiss on the cheek. *God, no.*

They hugged. Gaia disappeared into the back of the cab.

Loki stood in front of Compagno's, watching the taxi drive away. Tom knew he could make a move now. It would be so easy. His legs tensed. But right at that moment a black Mercedes pulled up beside the curb. Loki ducked inside. Seconds later the car's taillights vanished around a corner—gone before Tom could even exhale.

He had lost them.

They were gone. Both of them. Loki *and* Gaia.

And now Tom had to go back to his motel and pack a bag. He had no choice. If he didn't, he was a dead man. The reality was as clear as the snow falling around him: For the time being, all he could do was pray that George would be able to protect her.

It wasn't much to believe in.

She felt a
tremor of
rage.
Another
life lost
because
of some
stupid
white
powder.

flat mask

AS A RULE, GAIA DIDN'T TAKE CABS.

Proverbial Chatty Cathy

But Uncle Oliver wouldn't take no for an answer. He'd handed her a twenty-dollar bill and practically shoved her into the backseat. On the other hand, she could get used to this kind of treatment. Expensive meals, fancy cars . . . She drew in her breath. She'd better *not* get used to it.

But Oliver was going to make it. Of course he was. He was strong. Like her.

At least the driver wasn't in a chatty mood. There was way too much going on in her head to make small talk about the Knicks or listen to a litany of complaints about the mayor. Walking home through this snow—now an official blizzard—would have been far from pleasant, even for her. And the streets were absolutely deserted. She wouldn't even have been patrolling for muggers, rapists, and murderers.

"Stop here," Gaia instructed the driver. He pulled up to the curb and pointed to the meter. She handed him the twenty. "Ten back, please."

He silently counted out the bills—all ones, naturally—and thrust them into Gaia's hand. "Have a good night."

A freezing cold blast of air and snow hit Gaia's face as she slid out of the taxi. She sprinted toward the lobby of Sam's dorm. Never before had she been so anxious to see him, to talk to him . . . ever. For a second she considered creating a distraction to get past the security guard. But then she realized that this was just instinct—an instinct from the past. There was no reason to do so. She wasn't sneaking around anymore.

She burst through the doors. "I'm here to see Sam Moon," she breathlessly announced.

He glanced up from whatever sporting event was playing on his tiny black-and-white television set and grunted. A flicker of recognition crossed his chubby face. He nodded. The gesture filled Gaia with a strange wistfulness. She'd been here so many times now in the past few days that he knew her. She was part of the place.

And now she was leaving.

As she pounded up the stairs, Gaia categorized the things she wanted to tell Sam in order of their importance. There was so much, she didn't know where to begin. Clearing the second flight, she realized that her personality had taken a complete 180-degree turn. In the past no one, including Sam, could have pried her thoughts out of her. Not even with torture. Now she was practically bursting to share, share, share. She was a proverbial Chatty

Cathy. In some ways it was pathetic. In others it was liberating.

At last Gaia burst into the suite. It was as hot inside as it had been cold outside. The radiator in Sam's dorm was on overdrive.

"Sam!" she called, knocking on the door. "It's me."

"Come on in."

She stepped inside, then froze. He was lying in bed, wrapped in a blanket that looked like it had been first used during the Civil War. It was ridiculous. But there was no time to talk about *that*.

"Don't say anything," she ordered. "I have all this . . . stuff . . . to tell you. Just let me tell you the whole thing before you interrupt."

Sam blinked. He swallowed, then shrugged, sliding over to make room on the bed. But she remained standing. There was too much excess energy swirling inside her for her to sit.

"I told you about my uncle Oliver. But I didn't tell you the whole truth. Before we, well, you know, Oliver and I talked about leaving the country together, my life at George and Ella's was total hell, I hated school, and you were out all lovey-dovey with Heather." She took a deep breath, struggling to keep her thoughts straight. Sam's face was a flat mask, a *tabla rasa*.

"I wanted to move in with him, but I couldn't," she continued. "Not until I turned eighteen. But we realized that if we just moved to Europe for a few months, there would be no problem. It wasn't like George was going to bother to track me down."

Gaia paced back and forth across the tiny room. The radiator was clanging so loudly that she could barely hear herself think. But she had to get through this. She had to tell Sam about Oliver's illness. It wouldn't be real until she had said the words out loud.

"Anyway, I went to dinner with my uncle tonight, and I told him I didn't want to leave New York after all. But then he told *me* something. He has cancer. And his only hope for beating this thing is going to Germany to get some kind of experimental treatment." She paused, staring at Sam. "I don't know what to do. Should I stay here? Or should I leave?"

Sam took a deep breath. His expression was still unreadable. "Gaia . . . I—I'm sorry. Really." His voice was a flat monotone.

For the first time since she had walked into the room, Gaia noticed that Sam's skin was as white as a sheet. But she had the sense that he wasn't just upset about the idea of her moving away. His eyes were red, as if he had been crying.

"What is it? What happened?" she demanded, growing more and more disturbed by his glazed expression. It was as if he wasn't even there.

"Mike," Sam croaked.

Gaia knelt beside the bed and took his hands. "What about him?"

Sam shook his head. "He's . . . dead."

Several seconds passed before the words even registered. Gaia swallowed. A vision of Mary flashed through her mind. She felt a tremor of rage. Another life lost because of some stupid white powder. Of course, she hadn't really known Mike Suarez. She had seen him a few times when she had been stalking Sam's dorm, but he was basically a stranger. Still, Sam had told her all about him. Sam had liked him. Sam had befriended him. And now he was gone—*poof!* Just like that. It was so meaningless.

"Sam, I'm so sorry," she murmured. For the third time today she had absolutely no idea what to say.

"I went to the hospital to give him these magazines," Sam whispered, producing a rumpled stack of sports mags from under the covers. "But by the time I got there, he was gone." His voice broke. "There was nothing . . ."

Gaia wrapped her arms around Sam and pulled him close.

"It's okay to cry," she whispered as he shook against her. "It's good to cry."

But all she could think was: *It's too bad my words aren't true for myself.*

Ninety-Nine Percent Sure

"I WISH I HAD CABLE IN MY room," Heather mumbled into the phone, lazily twirling the cord around her fingers. "The idea of going into the living room and watching Nick at Nite with my parents is totally unappealing."

"I wish I had *you* in my room," Ed replied. "I'm lying in bed, looking at your picture."

"What are you wearing?" Heather asked.

"Hey, isn't that my line?" He started breathing heavily. It sounded like he was snoring.

Heather giggled. Thank God for Ed. He kept her sane. "Why don't we have breakfast tomorrow?" she suggested. "I'll come over to your apartment and make you my famous eggs Benedict."

"You don't know how to make eggs Benedict. You don't even know how to make toast."

"Okay. So I'll pick us up a couple of lattes at Starbucks and pour us two bowls of cornflakes."

Ed sighed. "Actually, I can't do breakfast tomorrow. In fact, I'm not going to be in school . . . for a few days."

Heather frowned. *This* was news. "What do you mean?"

"My mom is dragging me to my great-aunt's in

upstate. She broke her hip, and Mom has to help her out. But since they can't stand each other, I've got to be there as a human buffer zone."

For some reason, Heather was under the impression that Ed's great-aunt lived in Arizona with her third husband. But that must have just been a mistake. Or maybe she'd moved. No . . . Heather was sure now. She remembered Ed talking about her.

"It totally sucks," Ed added. "But I'll call you in a couple of days, okay?"

He was lying. It was obvious; Heather knew that much from the weird tone of his voice. But why? What could he possibly have to hide from her? She knew that Ed wouldn't cheat on her or hurt her in any way. At least, she was ninety-nine percent sure. If he couldn't tell her why he was leaving town, he must have a good reason. Unless it had something to do with . . .

No. He and Gaia are friends. Not even. They barely hang out anymore. Ed's moved past her. She was just an unfortunate episode in his mixed-up life.

"So . . . ah, I'll see you in a bit, okay?"

"Okay," she whispered. "Bye."

"Bye."

Heather hung up. Maybe this wasn't such a bad thing after all. She would have time to hang with her friends. They could go window shopping in SoHo or try to spot celebrities at Universal Diner. Except . . .

that Heather didn't want to hang out with her friends. Next to Ed, they were just shallow vessels with good skin and great haircuts.

She laughed out loud. Okay. That wasn't very fair. What was she thinking? She *loved* her friends. Yes. In fact, she was going to call one of them right now. Why not? It was time to start being Heather Gannis again.

Reasons for Gaia to Go

1. She wants to get to know her uncle.
2. Her uncle needs her.
3. They make really good sausages in Germany.
4. It's not forever. She'll be back.
5. If she weren't here, I could concentrate on my classes.
6. Without Gaia around, I wouldn't feel the need to blow my money on a new comforter.

Reasons for Gaia to Stay

1. She could finish her senior year.
2. I'll die if she's out of my sight for over six hours.
3. She barely knows her uncle. How much can she really care about him? (Admittedly, this is a self-ish, self-interested reason.)
4. If she moved to Germany, she wouldn't be able to survive without a steady diet of Krispy Kreme doughnuts.
5. I'll die if she goes. That deserves to go on the list twice.

I am going to go to Germany with Uncle Oliver. I am leaving town.

No matter how many times I say that, it still doesn't seem real. I enjoy irony as much as the next girl, but this is out of control. For years I drift from foster house to foster house, speaking only to stray dogs and hustlers and homeless people begging for change. Then I land in New York, where I actually make what would pass under the dictionary defini- tion as friends.

There's Ed. Definitely a friend.

Then there's Mary. She is—was— the only person who I ever allowed to paint my toenails, besides me. Now I wish I had admitted to her that I liked it. And I wish Mary were still alive. I think about her every day, along with my mother and all of the other people who were ripped from my life without giving me a chance to say good-bye.

And I find out I have an uncle

who actually wants to be a part of my life. Surprise! He's dying of cancer, and the only way I can spend time with him is to leave behind my new, real life—drumroll, please—boyfriend.

There isn't really a decision to make. I can't let down Oliver because I'm on a quest to lose my virginity. Or because Sam makes me feel like the star of a cheesy long-distance commercial. Or even because I think I might keel over and die if I have to spend a day away from him.

I don't get it. If the choice is so obvious, then why am I having such a hard time making it? The girl who has always fled suddenly wants to stay put—just when she's got a legitimate reason to go. Now, that's ironic.

<u>Memorandum</u>

To: BFF

From: L

Secure the following:

1. Hidden cameras at points *A*, *C*, and *F*.
2. Wardrobe—white gowns, white pants, white paper shoes.
3. Alarm system. Change all codes for purposes of security, then call me with the new one.
4. Hang photographs in subject's room. Include the picture of the Empire State Building I shipped last week.

Subject and I will arrive in Frankfurt within the week. Contact me about any potential glitches. There can be no mistakes.

There was no reason to draw a simile or fantasize. At this instant, life was wonderful.

that first domino

The Moth and the Bonfire

NEW YORK CITY HAD BEEN TRANS-formed. The grimy sidewalks were blanketed with over thirteen inches of clean, white snow, and even the air smelled fresher. Gaia knew that by this evening, the snow would turn to slush. There would be dirty footprints and dark yellow streaks from the thousands of dogs (and people) who used the streets as their lavatories.

But right now—before stores were open and before millions of commuters tramped their way through Manhattan—the city was beautiful.

It reminded her of winter mornings of her childhood.

White powder sprayed out from beneath Gaia's combat boots as she picked up her pace. Ozzie's Café was just up the street, and her sixth sense told her that Sam was already there, waiting for her. She could picture him reading the front page of *The New York Times* and sipping a cup of hot black coffee. Gaia stopped in front of the window. There he was. Sitting in a corner booth. The newspaper was spread out in front of him. She knocked on the pane and waved.

"Hi," he mouthed.

Gaia nearly tripped over herself as she rushed

inside to sit next to him. This whole relationship was starting to verge on pathetic. Well, at least comic. *I mean, look at me,* she thought. When she used to see other couples sitting side by side rather than across from each other, she'd always wanted to gag. But now . . . now she understood the need to be in physical contact with another human being at all times. She felt like a moth. And Sam was her roaring bonfire. She couldn't *help* but be drawn to him.

Okay, so maybe it wasn't so comic. Maybe it was just sad. Especially given the circumstances.

"How are you?" she asked. "Did you sleep after I left?"

He shrugged. "I dozed off for a while around four o'clock. I sort of spent the night having a one-way conversation with Mike."

Gaia nodded. She could definitely relate.

"I've been thinking," Sam began unceremoniously. "You should go to Germany."

His voice was completely devoid of emotion. But maybe that was only because he was struggling so hard to control himself. At least, that was what she *hoped* it was. "Your uncle Oliver is the only family you have. At least right now. And if you don't take this chance to know him, you'll regret it for the rest of your life—"

"Will you be here when I get back?" she found herself blurting out.

It was the question that had dogged her since Uncle Oliver had announced his diagnosis. Leaving Sam was one thing. She liked to be alone every now and then. Even for long stretches of time. But not knowing whether or not she could come back to him ... that was something else entirely.

Sam took her hand. His fingernails were bitten, their jagged edges rough against her skin. He was a wreck. "I'll wait for you. I promise."

"Really? I mean, not to sound callous or anything, but years of cynicism haven't done wonders for my innate ability to trust."

Fortunately Sam cracked a smile—which was her exact intention. "Really. Look, how's this? Instead of that cross-country camping trip this summer, I'll come visit you in Germany for a few weeks."

She withdrew her hand from his and extended it over the table for a formal shake. "Deal?" she asked, cocking her eyebrow.

He hesitated. "You know, this works both ways," he said, suddenly very serious. "If I wait for you, you *have* to come back to me. Otherwise I'll have to find you. And kick your ass. *I'll* learn kung fu, too, if I have to. Got it?"

All at once Gaia's eyes began to sting. She blinked rapidly several times. It was by far the most romantic thing anyone had ever said to her. No, it was the *only* romantic thing everyone had ever said to her. There was no reason to draw a simile or fantasize. At this instant, life was wonderful. She nodded, not trusting herself to speak.

"Good," he said. He took her hand, then brought it to his lips.

ACCORDING TO THE LOCAL MORNING

Of the Utmost Importance

newscaster, Kathie Lee was ensconced in another scandal and there was a new bra on the market that guaranteed both comfort and cleavage. Tom couldn't believe that with all of the news in the world, *this* rated top billing. No wonder no one cared about peace in the Middle East or famine in Africa. They were all too busy debating the Disney-fication of Times Square.

"Get to the weather!" Tom yelled at the television set. If this run-down dump had cable, he could switch to The Weather Channel. But Tom rarely stayed in motels that had TV sets, much less satellite dishes.

His cell phone rang just as the image on the screen changed to a man in a plaid blazer standing in front of a map of the United States. The guy promptly slapped a fake storm cloud in the general area of New York.

"It's bad out there, folks," the weatherman boomed. "Get out the hot chocolate and zip up your coats!"

Tom pushed mute on the remote control, then answered his phone. "Yes."

"All of the airports are closed, Tom." He didn't recognize the voice, but he often didn't. "No planes can come in or go out."

"I suspected as much."

"We'll let you know when we've got the all clear. Don't go anywhere."

In the past, Tom had held a strong conviction that the work he did for the government was of the utmost importance. He saved lives on a daily basis. But what did all of that mean if his bosses couldn't even guarantee the safety of his only child?

Tom grabbed his overcoat and a black wool cap. They might be able to order him to leave the country. But they couldn't stop him from checking on his own daughter when she was just miles away. They had his number. They'd find him. They always did.

SAM STRUGGLED TO KEEP HIS EYES

open as Dr. Witchell droned on about the inner workings of the small intestine. Man. He should have dropped this class when he'd had the chance. He was already two chapters behind in the reading, and he had three labs to make up. So far, this semester wasn't going any better than the last one.

Private Mantra

But it's not my fault.

It had become his private mantra, his litany. He'd repeated those five words to himself over and over again—a thousand times since he'd thrown up in that hospital, a *million* times. And yet he still didn't believe them. Mike's blood was on his hands. And all because Sam Moon had slept with Ella Niven. Or whatever her name really was. Sam had knocked over that first domino that sent the others tumbling . . . culminating in a boy's death. True, Sam hadn't known how insane Ella was when he had slept with her. True, he hadn't known what lengths she would go to in order to blackmail him. But that wasn't the point. There was only one point. Mike Suarez was gone.

"Mr. Sam Moon?"

His eyes popped open. He hadn't even realized they were closed. The blood instantly drained from his face. The lecture hall door was open. Dr. Witchell was talking to two men in blazers and khakis who were walking into the classroom. One of them was glancing at a small notebook. Both wore badges.

"Mr. Sam Moon?" the guy with the notebook called.

Detective Mantis. It had to be. Sam's stomach clenched. This was bad. One hundred and thirty pairs of eyes turned to stare at Sam as he heaved himself out of his seat. His legs felt like Jell-O. They were barely capable of supporting his body. *Be cool,* he told himself. *Routine questioning. That's all.* The guys were probably questioning all of Mike's suite mates and friends. It was part of a standard investigation.

"Come along, Mr. Moon," the professor said. There was no hiding the disdain in his voice. "You can get the notes from one of your classmates."

Sam forced himself to follow the two guys out into the hall. Would they make him take a polygraph test? If his sweaty palms and quaking knees were any indication, he would flunk. But he didn't do anything wrong. Not technically, anyway. Morally, yes—but legally, no. So there was no reason to be nervous.

"What's this about?" Sam asked once the door was closed.

"I'm Detective Katz," the one with the notebook

said. He had small beady eyes and a comb-over. "This is Detective Reilly. We'd just like to ask you a few questions. We'd like you to come to the station house with us."

His pulse instantly tripled. He could feel his shirt clinging to his back. "Does this have something to do with Mike Suarez?" he asked. His voice was hoarse.

Detective Reilly, who looked like he spent all of his off-duty time at a local pub, nodded. "Yes. It does."

A thought occurred to him. "Wait, where is Detective Mantis?" he asked. "I thought he was the guy handling the investigation."

The two guys exchanged a puzzled glance.

"Detective Mantis?" the comb-over asked. "Never heard of him."

"But . . ." Sam figured there wasn't much point in protesting. Whoever Mantis was, he wasn't here now. So Mike must have gotten the name wrong. He had been pretty out of it when Sam talked to him. Unless . . . unless Mike *hadn't* gotten the name wrong. Maybe the guy who had shown up in Mike's hospital room hadn't been a detective at all. The guy could have been connected to Ella somehow. Which meant that she had reached out from her grave to screw Sam all over again.

The knot in his stomach was starting to feel more like a noose.

166

HEATHER GRABBED THE APPLE SHE

Sick Aunt Story

had stashed in her locker, then slammed the door shut with far more force than necessary. She was only a few hours into her first day of school minus Ed, and it was a disaster. She was suddenly out of the loop.

Just like that. When she had asked Megan and Ashley if they wanted to see a movie tonight, they had looked at her like she'd asked if they wanted to go to a Barry Manilow concert.

It didn't matter, though. She'd win them back. After all, she had *made* their image. Without her those girls were just a bunch of giggling morons with ten thousand dollars' worth of rhinoplasty between them.

Besides, Heather Gannis had never begged for anything. She wasn't about to start now.

To top things off, Heather now spotted Gaia lumbering in her direction. Her perfect day was about to get even better.

"Hey, Heather," Gaia said. It probably the nicest thing she'd ever said to Heather up until this point in their lives. "Have you seen Ed?"

I could walk away, Heather thought. She could refuse to dignify Gaia's question with an answer and simply flounce down the hallway. But that might be perceived as a sign of weakness, and Heather couldn't afford to let any of her soft skin show.

"I don't keep tabs on Ed, Gaia. He's a big boy."

"Can we cut the verbal combat for two minutes? I really need to talk to him."

"Ed isn't in school today."

"Oh." Gaia pivoted and took off in the opposite direction.

This could be fun, Heather thought. "Don't bother going to his apartment," she called.

Gaia turned around, clearly miffed that Heather had guessed where she was heading. "So where is he?"

"He had to leave town for a few days. It's a family thing." She smiled. "I guess he forgot to tell you."

Gaia narrowed her eyes. "Are you telling me the truth?"

"Why would I lie?" Heather turned and walked away before Gaia could respond.

So. Ed didn't care enough about his precious friend to tell her that he wasn't going to be around. It looked like she had nothing to worry about. So what if his sick aunt story was lame? Whatever reason Ed had for being away clearly had nothing to do with Gaia Moore. That's what Heather called good news.

Detective Reilly:

State your name and age, please.

Sam Moon:

Sam Moon. Age twenty.

Detective Barnard:

What do you know about the death of your friend Mike Suarez, Sam? Do you mind if I call you Sam?

Sam Moon:

Uh, yeah. Sure. Call me Sam. The night Mike OD'd, I came home and went to bed. When I eventually came out of the room, I found Mike with a needle sticking out of his arm. I couldn't wake him up, so I called 911.

Detective Reilly:

What were you doing that night? Before you came home?

Sam Moon:

I, uh, went to a movie at the Angelica.

Detective Reilly:

Were you with anyone?

Sam Moon:

No, I was alone.

Detective Katz:

What was the movie?

Sam Moon:

Uh, let's see. I can't really remember the name
of it. Something foreign. There were subtitles.

Detective Reilly:

Uh-huh.

Detective Katz:

Had Mike done heroin before, to your knowledge?

Sam Moon:

Well, he partied a lot. But, ah, no. I don't
think so.

Detective Katz:

How about you, Sam? Have you ever used heroin?
Speed? Cocaine?

Sam Moon:

No. No. Never.

Detective Reilly:

Can't you tell us anything, Sam? Mike was your
suite mate. You guys probably shared a lot
together.

Sam Moon:

I'm sorry. I wish I could help, but I really
don't know anything. . . .

Detective Katz:

Okay. That's fine. Jut relax, Sam. Okay?

It was easy for Loki to say that because he saw on her face that her decision was final. This was it. A battle had been won.

two sides of the same coin

LOKI CHECKED THE TIME ON HIS

Rolex. Gaia was due in less than two minutes. He hoped that she had come to a decision— the *right* decision. It would be so unpleasant if he had to take extreme measures to convince her to leave the country with him. That wasn't how he intended for them to embark on their new life together.

Mindless, Spineless Trolls

To that end, Loki had brushed his robust face with a grayish powder he had ordered especially for the occasion. He had also enhanced the circles under his eyes with expensive stage makeup. It was crucial that he look his part. Loki wanted Gaia to respond as viscerally as possible to his . . . "condition."

When Gaia had suggested they meet in the park, Loki had readily agreed. He had assumed that on a day like today, the area would be deserted. Who ventured outside in this weather, even if the snow *had* stopped? But he had assumed wrong. The park was filled with college students and mothers with their young children, all building snowmen and snow forts and engaging in snowball fights.

Trolls, he thought. *Mindless, spineless trolls.*

He guessed that no one in his vicinity knew how to

order a bottle of fine wine or understood the delicate taste of sea urchin or could argue intelligently about the decline of opera in the twentieth century. Of course not. But that was a part of his mission: to educate Gaia about the more subtle pleasures in life. A small part, yes, but a crucial one. Tom had taught Gaia much—how to fight, how to speak many foreign languages, even philosophy and physics and history.

Still, even Katia hadn't bothered to teach Gaia how to carry herself in a couture gown. Gaia had never had a lesson in diction or etiquette. Loki would take it entirely upon himself to guide her through the final stages of her education.

When he was finished, she would be beyond perfection. *There!*

As always, when he caught sight of Gaia, his breath quickened. She was strolling through that pale imitation of the Arc de Triomphe that marked the entrance to the park. Yes, she definitely had to learn how to dress. No more of those brown painter's pants, sweatshirts, and combat boots. No. She would trade those in for velvet dresses. . . .

He stood and waved to her.

She smiled and quickened her pace.

"Gaia! You're lovely as always," Loki greeted her.

As she approached, he watched her take in his newly haggard appearance. The disguise worked. The concern in her eyes was real . . . poignant.

"How are you feeling?" she asked, sitting beside him.

"It's been a little rough these past few days," he said quietly. He coughed for several moments into his hand. "But don't worry yourself about me."

"Well . . . thanks for meeting me." Her eyes flickered over his face, her forehead creased with worry. "You probably shouldn't be out in the cold like this—"

"It's all right," he murmured.

She nodded, then took a deep breath. "Look, I want to come with you. I want to move to Germany. At least for the time being."

Loki exhaled. His heart hadn't felt this full since Katia was alive. "Are you sure, Gaia? I don't want you in any way to feel that I've pressured you into making this journey with me."

It was easy for Loki to say that because he saw on her face that her decision was final. This was it. A battle had been won. A battle as decisive as Midway. Winning the war was in his grasp; he could *taste* it. Years of hard work and tedium had culminated in this one joyful moment. Now their paths would converge for good.

"I'm positive." She paused. "So . . . when do we leave?"

Her voice caught on the last word, but Loki pretended not to notice. He didn't want to make the girl self-conscious. There were a few loose ends he had to take care of before leaving the city. Much of it—getting rid of the apartment, disposing of certain items, making arrangements—he could leave to his underlings. Some matters, however, he needed to handle personally.

"We can leave in two days," he told her. "That will give you time to get yourself organized."

"Two days," she repeated. For a split second she looked almost like a prisoner, a wild animal trapped in a snare. Then her features settled into resignation.

"Gaia, it is imperative that you don't tell anyone about our plan," Loki stated. "I know you won't tell George Niven. But it's also important that you don't mention it to any of your friends."

"Why? They won't try to stop me—"

"Our situation is very, very delicate," he interrupted gently. "Your friends might mean well, but not all young people have your keen sense of discretion."

"But—"

"Trust me, Gaia. As soon as we are in Germany, you can call and write your friends as much as you like. I'm sure that when they hear the circumstances, they'll understand." He gave her an intense stare. "They wouldn't really be your friends if they *didn't* understand, now, would they?"

She stared back at him, her eyes narrowing. "I . . . guess not."

Loki coughed a few more times for good measure, then laid a hand on Gaia's shoulders. "You have no idea how happy you have made me, my dear. Regardless of what happens with my illness, I will find great peace with you at my side." He pulled her into a hug. "This is going to be a wonderful time. For both of us."

GEORGE CHOKED BACK THE HACKING

cough that had plagued him since last night. He had woken up with a slight fever. Keeping an eye on Gaia all day had done nothing to improve his health. Not that he particularly cared. Life meant little to him now. He could drop dead of pneumonia

Bogus Illness

within a week and be thankful for it. But protecting Gaia, sparing her from danger . . . *that* had to sustain him. It was all he had left.

Hidden behind one of the two pillars of the miniature Arc de Triomphe, he fastened his gaze on Loki and Gaia. The man's resemblance to his friend was horrifying. Obviously—they were twins. But he couldn't separate the two in his mind. Loki *was* Tom, in a way. And vice versa. They were two sides of the same coin, only they had chosen opposite paths. And Gaia was at the crossroads.

The tiny microphone that George had sewn into the lining of Gaia's messenger bag was emitting a bit of static, but he could still hear their conversation clearly enough.

". . . love Germany," Loki was saying.

"What about . . ."

Damn, George thought. He adjusted the earpiece.

". . . word that you'll keep this between the two of us?" Loki asked again.

"Yeah. Of course." Gaia sounded so trusting, so naive.

"I'll call you with the details of our departure," Loki assured her. "Anything that you don't bring with you, we'll buy in Germany. I plan to make sure you have everything your heart desires——"

"All I want is for you to get well. If the experimental treatment works, I'll be totally and completely happy. . . ."

George shook his head. So that's how Loki had convinced her. He had made up some bogus illness. He'd probably convinced Gaia that he might have just weeks or month to live. George wasn't surprised. There was no level to which Loki wouldn't stoop to get what he wanted. But something had to be done. Gaia's life was at stake. Loki was taking her out of the country. There was only one solution: He would get in touch with Tom immediately and pray that his old friend was still in the city. If anyone would know how to proceed, it would be Tom—the man who knew Loki almost as well as Loki knew himself.

Two sides of the same coin, he reminded himself. He coughed again and hurried from the park.

SAM PICKED UP THE PLASTIC FOAM

cup of black coffee that sat before him on the ancient brown table in the interrogation room. He had consumed almost a quart of the muddy black liquid over the past hour, and he was starting to feel a buzzing in his head from the caffeine overload. He couldn't sit still.

A Real Nice Kid

"I really wish I could help you," he said for what must have been the tenth time. "But Mike's death is as big a mystery to me as it is to you."

"I understand all that," Detective Katz said. "All I want to know is this: Do you have a ticket stub from that movie you went to see, Sam?"

He stared down at the cup, nearly crushing it in his grip. Why had he told them he'd gone to the Angelica that night? It had been an idiotic thing to do. Sam *hadn't* done anything wrong. Nothing legally wrong, anyway. But his sense of self-preservation had kicked in, and he had heard himself say whatever would most distance himself from Mike and that poisoned needle. It made him sick. He was smarter than that.

"Um . . . I don't know," he finally mumbled. "I'll check all of my pants pockets when I get back to the dorm."

The detectives smiled at each other. They did that a lot. Like two lovers, sharing a private moment. Every time it happened, Sam felt an urge to jump up and smash their skulls together.

"You seem like a real nice kid," Detective Reilly said. "You go to a good college. You've got a pretty girlfriend. You're living the American dream, kiddo."

Sam nodded, unable to look at anything but the cup. His body was so tense, he thought he'd explode. "Yeah," he croaked.

"So . . . it would be a real blow if something happened to mess with all of that," Detective Katz whispered. "I mean, if *I* were you, I'd do all kinds of things to keep my life from getting messy. Almost . . . anything."

"I don't *have* to do anything," Sam insisted, glaring at him. His eyes instantly fell back to the cup when he saw that smarmy smile. "It *isn't* messy."

Detective Katz leaned back in his chair. "Fine. I'll tell you what, Sam. We're going to let you go ahead and get back to class now. But we would sure appreciate it if you found that ticket stub for us."

Sam nodded. "I will," he lied, hoping he could hang on just long enough to get out of here before he puked.

"Good," Detective Reilly replied.

Both men grinned.

Sam stood up, so jittery that he knew they could see him shaking. Screw it. What did they expect? They'd plied him with coffee. Now he knew how those perps on *NYPD Blue* felt. These two knew he was hiding something. He could feel their eyes on him as he walked out of the small, dark room. But Sam was sure his secret was far from what they expected it to be. His story was too outrageous. They'd never prove a thing.

They don't know for sure Mike's death wasn't an accident, Sam assured himself. As long as the rest of their investigation led to a dead end, he would be safe. Because at this stage of the game, there was no way those guys would believe the truth. Especially when the one person besides him who *really* knew what happened was dead.

But Sam was fairly certain of one thing. The cops weren't through with him. He would be back here, in this stinky little room—and next time the interrogation might not end with Sam walking out.

TOM WRAPPED HIS SCARF AROUND

his face as he exited the Fourteenth Street subway station. He'd felt safe underground,

Breaking Up

cut off from the world by the dozens of feet of concrete. It was a false sense of security, of course. George's phone call had proved that beyond a shadow of doubt. And unlike his daughter, Tom was well acquainted with fear. It was an emotion he tried to suppress as much as possible, but to no avail.

Gaia was in danger. It was the worst kind, too, because she didn't know of its existence. The airports had reopened, and planes were taking off without incident. Tom had no doubt that his own pilot was at the airport and ready to start his engines at a moment's notice. *If* he could get there in time.

Tom shuffled among the throng of commuters. He envied them. He always had. These people—these *citizens,* as some of his more jaded colleagues called them—they were so blissfully ignorant of what really went on in the world. The woman next to him might be thinking about what to buy her son for his birthday. Perhaps the young man just in front of him was deciding whether or not to buy his date flowers tonight. It had been so long since Tom had the luxury of such mundane thoughts that he almost couldn't remember what it was like. Had he ever known?

Just as he'd suspected, the cell phone in his pocket began to vibrate. Again. The subway ride had provided him with *some* cover, a reasonable excuse to be out of commission—but it had bought him only a couple of minutes. In a very real way he was like a prisoner on death row, buying hours of his life at a time with desperate excuses. He wrenched the phone from his pocket and jabbed the talk button.

"Hello!" Tom shouted. "Hello!"

"Where have you—"

"What?" he yelled. "I can't hear you!"

"Report to the airport immediately—"

"I can't hear you!" Tom repeated.

"This is an order. Repeat. This is—"

"I'm breaking up," Tom said. "I'll wait for—" He cut the line and jammed the phone back into his pocket. It would take them a while to find him and kill him. But as he continued down the crowded street, he saw a woman moving slowly but surely in his direction—staring straight into his eyes. She was tall, plain, maybe 130 pounds, nondescript clothing . . . the kind of woman nobody would suspect. She blended perfectly into any crowd. She was invisible. And in an instant Tom knew that he'd been made. They'd been trailing him the whole time.

She stuck her hand deep inside her coat pocket.

Tom forced herself to tear his eyes from hers. He stopped short, pivoted, and sprinted across the street. He wasn't ready to face the Agency. Not yet. He had to stall—no matter what the cost.

Top-Ten Things I'll Miss
about New York

1. Buying the Sunday *New York Times* late Saturday night.
2. Saving the masses from pickpockets, rapists, murders, etc.
3. Spending a whole day walking from Wall Street to Harlem and then back again.
4. Winning money from unsuspecting assholes at the chess tables in Washington Square Park.
5. Buying used (read: stolen) books from guys on the corner.
6. Krispy Kreme doughnuts. Especially the chocolate glazed and the crullers.
7. Going for dim sum in Chinatown.
8. Ed Fargo's lame jokes. Okay, *everything* about Ed.
9. Kissing Sam Moon.
10. Everything else about Sam Moon. This includes but is not limited to holding hands,

talking, eating greasy diner
food, going to movies, riding
the subway, making snow
angels, running my fingers
through his hair, having sex
(this last is in anticipation
of the event, which I'm positive will take place before I
leave).

The implication
of what they
were about to do
dawned on him.
Gaia had never **five**
had sex.
She was **long**
going to
give him her **years**
virginity with
an open heart.

"GAIA, I CAN'T BELIEVE YOU MADE
that move!" Sam exclaimed.
"You're leaving your queen
wide open."

Gaia looked down at the
chess set Sam had given her
and studied the board. He was
right. It was the kind of amateur mistake she hadn't made in years.

"I guess I'm not in the mood for chess," she
admitted.

Sam knit his brow. "You? Not in the mood for
chess?" He carefully set the board on his nightstand,
leaving all of the pieces in place. "Wow. I never would
have thought it possible."

She tried to smile. But it was impossible, especially
since she could tell Sam's cheeriness was forced. He
was like an actor who had been onstage
one too many nights in a row. His costume
was wearing thin. And he didn't have to pretend for
her. She knew he was hurting. One of his friends had
just *died.* Of all the people in the world, Gaia could
probably relate to that better than most. She heaved
herself off the bed and walked over to the tiny dorm-
room window.

"What's wrong?" he murmured.

"I'm going to tell you something I shouldn't," she
started—but instantly regretted what she'd said,

186

realizing how ominous she sounded. "You have to swear to me that you won't tell a single soul."

He laughed. "You actually want me to *swear*? What, are we in second grade?"

"I'm serious." She fixed him with a hard stare. She was sick of maintaining this stupid charade. Both of them were hurting. They needed to show it. They needed to *share*. Yes. *Sharing* was her new favorite word, it seemed—the way *chocolate* had once been. She needed sharing in the same way she needed chocolate. It had taken her five long years of torture and pain and bullshit, but she knew that now. She was ready.

Unfortunately, she would have to break her promise to Oliver that she wouldn't tell anyone about their plan. But here in the room with Sam, she realized how misguided that promise had been. Oliver didn't *know* Sam. There was no way it could get back to him. He never needed to know the truth.

"What is it, Gaia?" Sam pressed. The cheeriness was gone from his voice.

She took a deep breath, turning to him. "I saw my uncle Oliver this afternoon. We're leaving for Germany in two days."

Sam's eyes widened. "*What?* That soon? But I—"

"He's sick, Sam."

His face sagged, like a tire that was slowly losing its air. "Sick?"

"Yeah . . . look, he'll be fine, though."

Sam was silent. But then he smiled again—only this time it was a *real* smile. "Maybe he won't be, Gaia," Sam whispered. "But I hope he is. And no matter what happens, I'll wait. I'll . . . always wait." He laughed sadly. "Besides, I'll call you so often that your uncle will be afraid you've got a stalker back in America."

She grinned. "Promise?"

"Promise."

Amazingly, for the first time since Uncle Oliver had told her about his condition, Gaia felt calm. Knowing that there was a future with Sam was like . . . well, like auto insurance. Maybe the car would crash, but the victims would be compensated.

She only hoped that there would be no victims.

"THANK GOD YOU'RE HERE," GEORGE hissed. His breath made a sickly cloud in the night air.

Tom nodded, shoving his hands deep in his pockets. He didn't like Alphabet City. He never had. But he understood its uses. Down here, in the heart of a high-crime neighborhood, riddled with

A Good Meeting Place

drugs and prostitutes and abandoned buildings, people would leave them alone.

"You may have saved Gaia's life," Tom whispered, instinctively scanning the area. Any good meeting place was only *relatively* safe. That was one of the very first lessons an agent learned. Or a terrorist, for that matter.

George coughed. "I think we should go to the higher-ups," he croaked, doubling over and holding his hand over his mouth. "They could step in . . . maybe call in a team—"

"No," Tom whispered violently. He paced the sidewalk, breathing hard. For the very first time in his life he could feel the stress beginning to wear at his frayed nerves. "I don't trust them. For God's sake—I was almost taken out today, George. Some woman on Fourteenth Street."

George stared at him. "You were almost . . ."

"Yes." Tom managed a weary grin for his friend. "Which means that I owe you more than you even know for your information. Just meeting with me can put your life in jeopardy."

"So what do you want—" George's voice broke off as he began to cough.

Tom patted his friend's shoulder. "You're sick. You need to take care of yourself, George. Running around in this condition wouldn't be a help; it would be a hindrance. Stay way from me. Get well."

George shook his head. "I don't know what's wrong with me. I just can't seem to catch my breath. . . ."

"It's okay." Tom hesitated, knowing that this might be the only chance he would ever have to thank George for all he'd done. "Look, George, I just want you to know . . . I'll never forget what you did for me and for Gaia. You're . . . you're the kind of friend people in our business rarely make."

George nodded, but he was coughing too hard to respond.

Tom cast one last glance at him, then hurried from the corner and vanished into the night. There was nothing left to say. It was time to take action.

SAM OPENED HIS MOUTH, BUT NO

words would come. The fact that she was leaving New York was finally sinking in. Gaia was *going*. He wouldn't see her in the park. He wouldn't see her waiting for him outside his dorm. He found that he was almost

No More Thinking

angry. How could she leave him—*now,* when he needed her most?

But her uncle needed her, too. More than Sam. He *knew* that. He couldn't add to her worries. And that meant that he couldn't tell her about his interrogation this afternoon. And he definitely couldn't reveal the truth about what Ella had done. He had committed plenty of selfish, thoughtless acts in the past. But this time he was going to stay his course. Gaia's happiness was what mattered most. If he were in any way responsible for keeping her from her uncle, he would never forgive himself.

So until she was gone from his sight, he would simply put the Mike situation out of his mind. There was no point in thinking about it, anyway. All he could do was wait. Wait until those detectives came knocking on his door again . . .

"I want to spend every single second I can with you until you're gone," he murmured. "I'll be chasing after your plane, waving good-bye."

Gaia smirked. "You can't chase the plane, remember? You're not supposed to know I'm taking off."

"Okay, then, I'll chase *another* plane as a symbolic gesture."

Before he knew it, Gaia lunged forward and kissed him. He almost felt like she was attacking *him*—the same way she had attacked those guys on the bridge. He was powerless against her. Not that he minded, of course. It was kind of a turn-on. She wrestled him down on top of his bed.

"I've waited for this for a long time," she whispered in his ear. "My whole life."

The implication of what they were about to do

191

dawned on him. Gaia had never had sex. She was going to give him her virginity with an open heart. Sam knew Gaia well enough to know that if she did something, she did it all the way, no regrets. So this would probably be the most mind-blowing, mind-boggling, mind-expanding event of his twenty years . . .

Which was why he couldn't do it.

Sam forced himself to pull away. "We should wait," he heard himself say. It was almost impossible to believe. But he knew he meant it.

Her face fell. She looked like she'd been slapped. "What? *Why?*"

He took her hand. "Gaia, if we make ourselves hold off, then think about how incredible it'll be when we do it when you come back. Or when I come see you in Germany. Waiting will give us both something to look forward to."

She laughed miserably. "Hey, Sam, let me tell you something, all right? I'm *tired* of looking forward to it."

"Just trust me, okay? For now."

"Do I have a choice?" Gaia groaned. She rolled over on top of him. "All right. I'll trust you. But that doesn't mean you're getting off of this bed."

He kissed her. "I hadn't planned to."

Sam smiled up into her eyes. But part of him felt sick. He didn't tell Gaia the real reason he didn't want to have sex. The real reason was because he was afraid. Once they had crossed that boundary, he wouldn't be able to let her go. He wouldn't *allow* her to take care of her sick uncle. And that would make him an asshole. Again.

HEATHER SLIPPED ON THE RED

Win the Lottery

wool gloves that Phoebe had knitted for her. It didn't matter that the right hand was twice as big as the left one. It didn't matter that the gloves were so ugly that Heather would never be caught dead in them. What mattered was that Phoebe had the strength to make them.

"I love them!" Heather lied. "These will go great with my black leather jacket."

Phoebe rolled her eyes. "Come on, Heather. They're pathetic. But Mariah promised she would teach me how to do a cross-stitch later this week."

So Phoebe really *was* making progress. She could see through Heather's bullshit. Heather had to laugh. Phoebe might still look like she had one foot in the grave, but she was getting better. Heather wouldn't have thought that someone that thin had the energy to crack a joke. Much less knit some crappy gloves. Or do anything else, for that matter.

"You know, it's funny," Phoebe continued, sitting up in bed. "A year ago I would have said that only freaks and neurotics talked to shrinks. But now I can't believe I went for so long keeping my feelings bottled up. Then again, I guess I *am* neurotic. So it makes sense."

Heather smiled. "You're not neurotic. You're an A-type personality. There's a difference."

Phoebe raised an eyebrow. "Okay. I've given you like five chances to diss me, and you haven't bitten. I know you're not holding back because of the anorexia. You insulted me plenty of times when I was in the hospital."

"I'm in a good mood," Heather said with a smirk. "Is that okay with you?"

"But why?" Phoebe insisted. "I mean, I know things are going well with Ed . . . but judging from the way Mom and Dad are acting, I didn't get the impression that things were so hunky-dory at home." She paused. "What's *with* them, anyway?"

Heather swallowed. She was wondering how long it would take before Mom and Dad came up. Phoebe was allowed a visit from one family member twice a week plus one meal out. Naturally, Mr. and Mrs. Gannis had gotten the first two turns. And naturally, when they had arrived home from the visit, they talked more about the cost of the treatment than about Phoebe's progress. Of course, that was all going to change. . . .

"That good, huh?" Phoebe joked in the silence.

"Things will finally start going right for our family," Heather informed her sister. "Trust me."

"Oh, yeah? How's that?"

Phoebe was no idiot. Even though the rest of them had tried to shield her from their stress over the rising hospital bills, she knew she was costing a fortune.

"Let's just say that you shouldn't worry about how long you need to spend recuperating here. It's not going to be a problem."

"Did we win the lottery?" she asked.

Heather smiled and looked her straight in the eye. "In a way . . . yes."

I've spent the past twenty-four hours trying to warn my daughter that she is in grave danger. That premise seems fairly simple on its face. If a man's daughter runs into the road, he runs after her. If his little girl seems like she's about to stick her finger in an electrical outlet, Dad rushes forward and pulls her away. Then he tells her in vivid, gory detail what will happen should she ever follow through on her curiosity.

But I haven't been able to come out of the shadows. I haven't been able to *be* a real father for more than five years now. She has seen me only once, when I saved her life. But I saw the doubt in her eyes that night. Her mind has been poisoned against me.

She doesn't know about the drawer full of letters I have written to her but have never been able to send. She doesn't know how lonely I am each and every day, longing for my daughter.

Nonetheless, I have tried to warn her. I have trailed her as closely as I can. But there are others in my way. Agents are trailing *me*. Every time I get close enough to Gaia to be able to call out—or even just look in her eyes—I feel them closing in. And then I have to flee and vanish into the bowels of the city until they are off my trail.

Because if they catch me, that will be the end of my effort.

I am effectively AWOL. I hope that soon Gaia will be safe, and I can resume my duties. But that may no longer be possible. Not unless I can find a way to trap Loki. Until he is locked up, no one will be safe.

So far, my approach to warning Gaia has been a failure.

And I cannot fail.

Ed glanced around the room, up at all the swirling faces in surgical **the** masks hovering **emptiness** over him. Yes, he was definitely in panic mode now.

THE SHEETS WERE COLD AND

Human Lab Rat

smooth against Ed's upper body. He wondered if he would be able to feel their texture against his legs when he woke up.

"Ed, you can still back out," Dr. Feldman informed him. "It's not too late."

Are you out of your freaking mind? The guy was unbelievable. "Trust me, I don't want to," Ed assured him. "I want to do this."

The doctor glanced at Ed's parents. "You all understand the risks?"

"Yes," Ed answered for them. Was the guy trying to talk him out of this or what? "You've told us everything that could go wrong. The operation might not work. The operation has a ten percent chance of causing even more damage to my spinal cord. Every surgery carries the possibility that the patient will never regain consciousness."

The statistics had been drilled into Ed's head a thousand times. His parents had even given their consent, signing a form that for all intents and purposes made him a human lab rat. So what if he lost the use of his arms? So what if he couldn't pee by himself anymore when he woke up? Ed didn't care. Maybe he would if he thought about it too hard—but at this moment he was resolved. He was already disabled. If the worst happened, he would deal with it.

But if the best happened . . . well, every big payday involved some risk.

Dr. Feldman nodded one more time at his parents.

His mom squeezed his hand, then leaned over to kiss him on the forehead. "We love you, sweetie."

"We'll be right here when you wake up, buddy," his dad added. "Be strong."

"Hey, chill out, people," Ed murmured, trying to lighten the moment. He glanced up at them from the gurney. "What's a little neurological damage among family?"

But his mom and dad did *not* look amused. They could at least try to *act* like they weren't as nervous as he was. Stone-faced parents didn't exactly inspire confidence.

"Let's go, Dr. Feldman," he urged. "This is going to turn into a Hallmark moment any second—and none of us want that."

"Whatever you say, Ed." The doctor opened the door to his hospital room, and half a dozen nurses, doctors, and orderlies streamed in.

Moments later Ed was being wheeled down the hall, heading at what felt like sixty miles an hour toward the OR. His heart pounded. Why did he feel like a prisoner on death row? This was about *freedom*. Not imprisonment . . . okay. Slow down. Now *he* was starting to think like a Hallmark card.

"Ed, this is Dr. Ramirez," Dr. Feldman announced, gesturing toward a guy who looked all of about eighteen. "He'll be assisting me."

"How ya doin', Ed?" Dr. Ramirez asked.

Ed forced a polite grin. But the fact of the matter was that he was verging on panic. What, did they have high school students doing operations now? Maybe this wasn't such a great idea. Maybe he *liked* being in a wheelchair. Maybe. Maybe. Maybe.

Please, God, I know I haven't spoken up for a really, really long time, but I need you to listen. I'm about to have a major *operation. You've got to watch my back. Please. Don't let anything go wrong. Please—*

What was the old saying about prayer? That it was the last refuge of the damned? Something like that . . .

"Ed, we've put the anesthesia into the IV bag already attached to your arm," Dr. Feldman explained. "You're going to start feeling drowsy in a few seconds."

Ed glanced around the room, up at all the swirling faces in surgical masks hovering over him. Yes, he was definitely in panic mode now. He'd heard horror stories, terrible things about people who didn't go all the way under. What if he could *feel* everything they were doing to him?

"I'm not getting tired," Ed protested, squirming. "It's not working—"

"Just start counting backward from a hundred for us, Ed," Dr. Feldman interrupted, holding Ed's arm. His eyes, hovering over Ed's face, looked serene and confident.

Ed tried to relax. "One hundred, ninety-nine, ninety-eight . . ."

Actually, the old doc had a point. All at once Ed's eyelids weighed a thousand pounds each. He felt like he had pulled an all-nighter and then wheeled the New York marathon.

". . . ninety-seven . . ."

I'm going to be better, Heather, he thought. Once he could walk, everything would be different. No more doubts or insecurities. He would be Shred again. The daredevil who knew no wave too big or any skate ramp too steep.

". . . ninety-six . . ." What was the next number? He couldn't remember the next number. ". . . ninety-three . . ."

Gaia's face materialized. She was smiling. She was telling him that everything was going to be okay—the surgery would be a success.

I love you, Ed thought. *No, wait! I love—*

Luckily at that moment he drifted into total darkness.

"MY CHICKEN MARSALA IS DELICIOUS,"

Pregnant Pause

Heather's mom proclaimed. "I think it's the best I've ever had."

"And the veal is wonderful," her dad added. "You should try to find out what spices the chef used."

"Good idea, honey." Heather's mom turned to Phoebe, obviously trying to look casual. "How is your salad, Feebs?"

Phoebe smiled politely. "It's delicious. Thank you."

Heather considered pointing out that her sister had taken approximately three bites of the Caesar salad with grilled chicken she had ordered. But why? They were all having a miserable enough time already. It was as if her family had been abducted and replaced with Mom, Dad, Heather, and Phoebe simulations. Their dinner conversation gave whole new meaning to the term *pregnant pause.*

Her parents were like frightened children, terrified of saying anything that might make Phoebe uncomfortable. Heather doubted that this particular scenario was what the therapists had in mind when they made all of their patients go out for dinner with their families. Then again, what did they expect? For the

Gannis family to be standing around a piano, singing show tunes and eating fried chicken dripping with fat? The Waltons they were not. They weren't even the Simpsons.

"Did anything interesting happen at school today, Heather?" Dad asked.

Heather racked her brain. "Uh . . . not really." This wasn't the prime time to bring up the fact that her so-called friends were treating her like a leper or that she had received a C-minus on her physics lab report.

"Is anyone going to want dessert?" Mrs. Gannis asked the table. "I hear the flan here is excellent."

At the mention of dessert Phoebe's face tensed, and Mr. Gannis's Adam's apple began to bob up and down. Heather knew what her father was thinking about. The bill. He had probably already calculated the cost of their entire meal, including tax and tip.

"I'm stuffed," Heather announced. "I'll have enough shrimp scampi left to eat it for dinner tomorrow night." That ought to make her dad happy. One less box of mac 'n' cheese consumed in the Gannis household.

"I'm full, too, Mom," Phoebe said. She made a show of putting one last bite of salad in her mouth. "This chicken is *really* filling."

Mom looked like she was about to cry. Dad looked like he was about to keel over from a heart attack at any second. Phoebe wasn't the only person at the table in need of a psychiatrist. Then again, *paying for a shrink would probably have sent her dad over the edge.* He was barely hanging on as it was.

Heather was tempted to announce to the entire family that Ed had offered to step in and help out with his millions. But parents were tricky. She was going to have to approach them in just the right way—and she hadn't figured out what that was yet. She wasn't even sure she was really going to go through with taking Ed up on his offer.

Part of her knew that it was wrong to depend on him that way, no matter how rich he was. But another part considered . . . maybe it wasn't. In fact, when Ed had brought up his fortune the other morning, it wasn't the first time that Heather had thought of it. She had been well aware that he had millions coming his way. She just hadn't known how *many* millions. . . .

But I didn't start going out with Ed again for his money, she reminded herself. That was what counted. It certainly hadn't been her motivation when she kissed him at his sister's engagement party. Of course not. That wasn't what Heather Gannis was about. No way.

The only thing was, she had no idea what else Heather Gannis *could* be about.

GAIA WAS HAVING A HARD TIME

concentrating. She was thinking about sex. Then again,
she figured she wasn't in the
minority. At any given time, it
would be safe to say that ninety
percent of the Village School's student body was thinking about sex.
Maybe she *was* really becoming a
normal teenager.

No Problem at All

Why the hell hadn't Sam
wanted to sleep with her last night? Her emotions kept
flaring from anger, to amusement, to frustration—
then back again to repeat the process, like some kind
of traffic light. Green, yellow, red.

Stop it! she ordered herself.

". . . part of the dramatic form," Mr. MacGregor
was saying.

She pushed the image of Sam's body out of her mind
and tried to listen to the lecture. Gaia had already been
reprimanded twice in the past twenty minutes for not
paying attention. She should probably at least *pretend*
that she cared about Sophocles, the Greek playwright.
But in reality, she'd already read most of his plays a long
time ago. Sophocles was one of her father's favorites.

It sucks that I have to go through with this charade,
she thought, making a show of scribbling in her notebook. In principle, she hated dishonesty

in any form. And being here was dishonest. But showing up for school had been part of the deal. Uncle Oliver had said that if she stopped going, even for a few days, it could mean another call to George. And that was intolerable—

There was a knock on the classroom door.

Mr. MacGregor frowned. He put down his chalk and opened the door a crack. A pimply hall monitor whispered something to him. Why was it that all hall monitors seemed to get off on their power to give illegally roaming students detention slips?

"Gaia, you're to report to the office," Mr. MacGregor suddenly announced.

Gaia blinked. She didn't know whether to feel wary or relieved. But any excuse to get out of *here* was fine by her. She grabbed her bag and coat and hurried to the front of the room. Could it be George again? Had he somehow figured out that she was planning to leave town? No. Not unless . . .

"I know—get the notes from someone after class," Gaia said automatically when she passed Mr. MacGregor. He gave her a look but turned back to the class without further comment.

"Do you know what this is about?" Gaia asked the hall monitor.

He shrugged. "I was told to get you out of class. And to give you this letter. It was left by a family member. The secretary in the office said it was urgent. . . ."

Gaia ripped open the envelope and pulled out a note. Not surprisingly, the guy didn't give her any space at all. Instead he stood right next to her, a creamy expression on his face. *Jesus.* One more thing *not* to miss about this school. She read quickly:

> *Dear Gaia,*
>
> *I know this is sudden, but there has been a change of plans. We must leave for Germany this afternoon. Leave school immediately and take a cab to the airport. We'll send for your things when we arrive at our destination. It is of the utmost importance that we leave on TWA flight 344 at 2:35 P.M. I know you thought you would have more time with your friends before we left, but for reasons I'll explain later, this is how it has to be. I will meet you at the TWA skycap station at JFK airport.*
>
> > *Love,*
> > *Uncle Oliver*

Also enclosed in the envelope was a passport for her. Gaia was numb. This was it. She wasn't going to be able to say good-bye to Sam . . . or even to patch things up with Ed. She was leaving New York today—right now.

She took a deep breath. Sam would understand. She would call him the minute they landed in Germany, no matter what time it was.

"Is there a problem?" the guy asked eagerly.

Gaia shook her head. "No. No problem at all."

She turned and strode down the hallway. Strange. This would be the last time she set foot in this hellhole of a school. She almost felt sad about it. But not quite.

Ed loved the ocean in the middle of July. He didn't even need his wet suit as he paddled out to sea. He felt as if he weighed ten pounds in the water. Total freedom.

He looked out toward the horizon, where the sun was beginning to rise. This was his favorite time of day. There were only a couple of other guys out this early. He felt as though he had the whole Atlantic Ocean to himself.

Ed pumped his arms faster, eager to be far enough from shore to catch one of the giant waves that had been rolling in since late last night. This was going to be a great day.

Suddenly Ed clutched his surfboard. What was he doing out here? He was crippled. Crippled guys didn't surf. Crippled guys weren't even supposed to be swimming in the ocean. He was defenseless.

Fear gripped him as he began frantically to flail his arms against the rising waves. No! He had to get out of here. But there were no lifeguards, and the closest surfer was too far away to see that he was in trouble. He was going to die.

First his left leg began to move. And then his right. Ed began to kick, faster and faster. He wasn't paralyzed! He could move, just like he always had.

He felt a flood of relief. The wheelchair had been part of some horrible nightmare. But now that he was awake, everything was all right again. He was whole.

Ed stood up on his surfboard just as a six-foot, white-capped wave headed for him. The wave rose beneath his board, and Ed was flying. . . .

GAIA FELT AROUND THE BOTTOM

Agonizing Slowness

of her messenger bag as the taxi neared John F. Kennedy International Airport. She needed to find quarters. Lots of them. The driver was going to be lucky if he got his full fare, much less a tip. The thirty-five-dollar ride was going to deplete all that remained of her meager savings. But she wouldn't need them anymore.

"What airline?" the guy barked.

"Uh . . . TWA," she answered distractedly.

He stepped on the gas, weaving through the five lanes of traffic that were circling the packed airport. The driver swerved in front of a huge SUV and jammed on the brakes.

"We're here," he announced.

Gaia thrust two fistfuls of fives and singles into his hand, then poured the change on top of it. "It's all there."

"Gee. Thanks, doll." He grunted, then gunned the engine as Gaia slammed the back door.

One more thing she wouldn't miss: cabdrivers.

Immediately she began scanning the crowd for Uncle Oliver. He was nowhere to be seen. She walked toward the skycap station. She had expected him to be at the little counter, waiting, but he wasn't there, either. *He probably got held up in traffic,* she decided. If it hadn't been for her kamikaze driver, she wouldn't have arrived for another fifteen minutes. She circled the skycaps as they tagged bags and sent them onto the conveyor belt. Still no sign of him. Minutes ticked by, plodding with agonizing slowness. The clock said 1:55. Their flight was in forty minutes. Didn't international flights require you to check-in an hour and a half early?

He's not going to show. He's not going to show up, and I don't even have a dollar-fifty for the subway. Terrific. She would have to hitch a ride from the kind of sleazebag that liked to give young, strange girls rides into Manhattan. Which probably meant she would end up in a fight . . .

Had she hallucinated this entire scenario? Maybe there *was* no Uncle Oliver. Maybe she was so desperate for the love of her family that she had invented him. Like that movie *Fight Club*. Only instead of beating herself to a bloody pulp, she ate at expensive Italian restaurants—

"Gaia!"

GEORGE WAS FEELING BETTER already. The doctor had given him a shot of penicillin and a prescription for a full run of antibiotics. If only he could heal as quickly mentally as he was physically . . .

A Pleasant Image

He tried not to think about the empty house. The house should have meant nothing to him, anyway. But the emptiness did. Ella was dead . . . not necessarily a bad thing. Gaia was getting out of school. Definitely a good thing. Of course, he always felt better when she was under this roof. But Tom had been clear that George shouldn't try to interfere with her normal routine. Her father probably had her under surveillance at this very moment—standing outside a diner window as Gaia ate cheeseburgers and french fries with her friends.

It was a pleasant image. George hoped it was also accurate.

He walked into the kitchen to get some water. He was going to fill a pitcher, then climb into bed with his electric blanket. The faster he recovered, the faster he would be of help to Tom.

But on his way out the door something caught his eyes. The light on the answering machine was blinking. George pushed the button, praying it wasn't a message from someone at the Agency, inquiring as to Tom's whereabouts. But they would never call this number. It wasn't a secured line.

"Hi, George. It's Gaia. Listen, don't worry about me. I just want you to know that I'm not going to be around for a while. But really, there's nothing to worry about. I'm fine. I'm only telling you because I don't want you to tear out your hair when I'm not home by midnight. I'll be in touch." There was a pause. Static filled the air. "And thanks, George. For everything."

The beep sounded. The message was over.

Loki got to her.

George couldn't move. His heart froze inside his chest. He was literally petrified. His feet were made of stone.

Loki got to her.

It was too late to do anything to stop him. George sank into a chair at the kitchen table and dropped his head into his arms. Hot tears rolled down his face. He had failed in his mission to protect Tom's daughter. He had failed in *everything.*

"NOW BOARDING FIRST-CLASS PAS-

sengers on flight 344 to Frankfurt, Germany," a voice boomed over the PA system. "All first-class and preferred passengers are welcome to board at any time." There was a crackle. "Also all of those passengers needing a little extra time."

One Last View

Uncle Oliver turned to her. Just being one step closer to the experimental treatment in Germany seemed to be having a beneficial effect on his health.

He looked far better than he had in the park yesterday. In his crisp, expensive suit and tie and elegant overcoat, he looked like a man without a care in the world.

"Ready, my dear?" he asked.

"Yep. Ready." She stood up and slung her messenger bag over her shoulder.

Uncle Oliver put his hand on her elbow and guided her toward the employee who was taking boarding passes.

"Good afternoon, sir," the woman said, taking the boarding passes from Oliver's hand. "Enjoy your flight."

"Thank you. We will." He led Gaia toward the long ramp that was attached to the door of the airplane.

"One second," Gaia burst out. She stopped in her tracks, and Oliver stopped beside her. "I just need to do one more thing."

She turned around and looked behind her. She needed one last view of New York from the ground—even if that view was of the inside of an airport.

"Okay, Uncle Oliver," she said. "*Now* I'm ready. Let's go."

Gaia turned back around and walked toward her new life. She had no idea when she would see Manhattan again. But she was doing the right thing. She was certain of it.